THE GIRL FROM PUERTO RICO

The Girl From Puerto Rico

by
Hila Colman

WILLIAM MORROW & COMPANY
New York, 1961

Fifth Printing, November 1970

For my sun-loving friend Sesyle and
all our friends in sunny Puerto Rico

THE GIRL FROM PUERTO RICO

Chapter 1

❧❀❧

Felicidad Louisa Marquez stretched out luxuriously on the hillside beside her house and lifted her face to the sun. She felt deliciously warm and earthy, the way she felt when she dug her toes in the sand at Luquillo, and an important part of her delight was knowing that it was forbidden. Sooner or later her mother would be calling out to her, "Stay out of the sun, Felicidad! Your face will get covered with freckles. The sun will ruin your complexion!"

What did a few freckles matter? Maybe she would just get tan instead, like the American *turista* who sat in the sun for hours. Nothing happened to their complexions!

Her complexion, however, was not what she had come out here to think about. She wanted to think about Fernando and the dance tonight, about the dress she was going to wear and whether her hair would come out right—and private thoughts too, about how it felt when he took her in his arms to dance and when, with

9

everyone else around, she suddenly found him looking at her intently.

Just thinking about it made her feel strange and different, nervous and excited, as if there were another person inside her whom she didn't know at all.

These were crazy thoughts for an ordinary September afternoon. Everything was the same as it had always been, and she was just Felicidad—she couldn't be two people. Her name meant happiness, and her mother said it was her special gift to bring happiness to people. Could she bring happiness to Fernando? She blushed furiously at such a bold thought, and hastily pulled her mind away from him.

There, only a few yards away, was the house she was born in, and nestled in the valley below was the village of Barranquitas, where she had lived all her life. She could see the cross on the church and the pale-pink stucco of its walls overlooking the plaza like a serene and steadfast guardian. The color of the church had the same glow as Sister Concepción's face, and the two always reminded her of each other. And there was the Collegio de Baptista and the green square of the plaza, with the pink and yellow stores and buildings grouped around it.

Nothing was different, not even the voices of her father and her brother Carlos arguing in the house! How many times had she heard them having the same discussion!

She could hear Carlos speaking now, his voice in the past few years having become deeper and stronger than her father's. "Why can't I go to New York? I could go next week with José and Luis. They have jobs waiting for them; I could have one too."

"You belong here, Carlos," her father answered.

He was too proud to say, "I need you," which was the truth, especially since the doctor had told him that his heart was weak. But Carlos' answer to that would be that he could send enough money home from New York for his father to hire help.

"We have six beautiful acres of bananas planted here. Isn't that enough for you?" Mr. Marquez continued.

"I don't want to be a farmer," Carlos said, his voice becoming impatient. "I want to make a lot of money. I can make money in New York, not here."

"Money, money! That's all you boys think about. It is beautiful here, quiet and peaceful; we have enough to eat, and we don't have gang wars and crazy kids running around with knives. It's a good life here. The *turista* from the States come here, because the sun is always shining. It should be good enough for you."

"You don't understand! You'll never understand!" Carlos' voice was hopeless and dejected, almost like a child's again—not like that of a big, strong eighteen-year-old man.

"I understand well. The farm is not good enough for

you. You want to be a big shot in New York. But maybe you won't like it there. Did you ever think of that? Maybe they won't receive you with open arms in New York."

"Oh Papa!"

Felicidad felt her body tensing as she strained to listen, and yet she wanted to shut her ears to their words. All thoughts of Fernando and the dance had floated off into the blue haze that was gathering around the hills. She felt as if she could not bear to hear this argument again. She loved them both so much, her father and Carlos, and when they fought this way, as they had been doing now for months, it made her frightened and sad.

Where would it end? Carlos was determined to get away from the small town in Puerto Rico where the family had always lived. That was all he talked about. Often at night, lying in bed awake on her side of the thin wall that separated her room from the one Carlos shared with their younger brother Willy, Felicidad trembled with fear that Carlos was furtively packing and would slip out in the night and be gone, far away, by morning.

Then she would say a quick little prayer for Carlos, and lie in bed, tense in the agony of not knowing. Was that little creak in the floor Carlos tiptoeing about? Was that small noise a bureau drawer being gently opened?

She couldn't bear it if Carlos went away, and it would surely break her father's heart, and her mother's too. She couldn't even bear to *think* about it. She and Willy would be lost without him. Besides, there wouldn't be anyone to chaperon her if Fernando should ask her out again! Carlos was a wonderful chaperon; her mother trusted him more than anyone. But still and all, he knew when to look the other way, and sometimes, when Fernando took her hand in his, Carlos never seemed to notice at all.

But that was a selfish and silly reason for not wanting Carlos to go away. She hoped she wasn't growing up to be a silly and vain person. Father Sebastian had talked to her and some of her friends only a short while ago, and some of the things he'd said made her worry about Carlos and about her own thoughts too.

"We must be on guard," he said, "against all the material wealth that is coming into our little island—the luxurious hotels and the fine factories that are being built. The United States is our good friend, but the people do not always walk with God. We must be careful not to lose our own way of life, our close family ties, our love of the earth, and our spiritual values."

Carlos must not go away and break up their family. The five of them belonged together, here at home in Barranquitas, where it was safe, and where all their cousins and aunts and uncles, their grandparents, and their friends lived too.

But did she want always to be safe? Did she want to live forever where it was the same day after day? New York was only a few hours away, and every day the planes were jammed with Puerto Ricans who didn't want just to stick on this little island forever. Carlos wasn't the only one who wanted to get away!

Felicidad did too! Wasn't Willy always teasing her about the way she pored over the magazines from the States? But even that wasn't enough. She wanted to see it all with her own eyes, to see the people and the buildings, the streets and the shops, all the wonderful places. . . .

"Felicidad, Felicidad!"

Her mother interrupted her thoughts. Felicidad pulled herself up quickly and ran into the house before her mother had a chance to scold her for sitting out in the sun. Anyway, there was a lot of work to be done, and she would have to help. Today the clothes had to be washed. Mrs. Marquez hated washing clothes. She had been brought up in a home with servants, and she had never quite recovered from the fact that she had fallen in love with a farmer who couldn't afford any. When the children were small, her husband had hired a young cousin to help out, but ever since Felicidad became old enough to help, Mr. Marquez preferred to save his money and spend it on a refrigerator, an electric stove, and a television set.

Their house was equipped with electricity, but the plumbing was very old-fashioned. There was an outside pump, where Felicidad had to fill the tub with water, and if she wanted it hot, she had to bring it into the house and heat it.

Now she looked around for Willy to help her carry the heavy tub of water, since by this time, her father and Carlos had gone out to the fields to cut the bananas. Willy was at the creek fishing, and Felicidad walked down to get him.

It was a beautiful day, a day for dreaming and sitting in the sun, not for working. She would have tried to put the washing off until tomorrow, except for the fact that she wanted to wash the ruffled white petticoat she'd wear under her organdy dress tonight. Perhaps she'd wear a hibiscus flower in her hair. . . .

Idly she watched a small, yellow-breasted bird fly across her path and alight on the *canario* vine her mother had growing on their fence. She could hear his shrill song, although he was now hidden among the yellow, trumpet-shaped flowers, which were bigger than himself.

What was New York really like? Felicidad wondered. Everything she'd heard about it and the pictures she saw in the magazines frightened her a little, but excited her enormously. It all seemed so glamorous! Carlos said you could go to a different movie every night and that there were hundreds of shops and places of amusement, with something exciting happening every minute!

Felicidad spotted Willy and sat down beside him. "Catch any fish?" she asked. He was the darkest one in the family, most of him constantly tanned by the sun. Now his bare legs and feet and his long, thin arms were only a few shades lighter than the earth he was sitting on. Next to Felicidad's fair skin he looked as if he belonged to a different family.

"Not yet, but I will," Willy said hopefully.

Felicidad stretched out on her back and gazed up at the sky. It was nice and cool in the shade underneath the trees. "Do you want to go to New York?" she asked, unable to push from her mind the thoughts whirling around in it.

Willy gave his sister a swift, alert glance. "If Carlos goes, I want to be with him." Then he shrugged his shoulders. "But I hope he stays here. I don't think I'd like a city. What about you? You wouldn't like to leave Fernando, would you?" he asked teasingly.

Felicidad blushed and tossed a pebble at her brother. "Fernando and I are nothing to each other but good friends," she said primly. "Besides," she added, with a faraway look in her eyes, "I'd like to meet some New York *americanos* before I settle down here in Barranquitas."

"You mean before you marry Fernando," Willy said with a grin.

Felicidad's eyes were dreamy. "Maybe," she said. "But I've never met any girls or boys except those who live in this village. Wouldn't you like to see something of the world before you settle down here?"

Willy dug his toes into the earth. "I don't know. I like it here."

"You're scared!" Felicidad said astutely. "You're like Fernando. I think he never wants to leave Barranquitas."

"What's wrong with that?" Willy retorted. "Even the New York *americanos* say it is the most beautiful place they ever saw. What's so great about leaving it?"

Felicidad did not answer. It was beautiful and safe here, and she did not want to leave Fernando. And yet, like Carlos, she was yearning to see for herself all the wonders of New York, which they had heard so much about. She had the feeling of being divided into two. Part of her wanted to remain in Barranquitas and live the way her parents and their parents had done. The hills were so beautiful! She loved to watch them in the early dawn from her bedroom window and see the sun come slanting through the haze, like the head of a golden-haired girl in a web of tulle, slowly lighting up the heavens with a pink glow. She loved the village nestled in the valley, especially in the afternoons, when all its many colors were etched clearly in the bright tropical sunshine. It was then that everyone gathered around in light frocks, and she and her girl friends would walk slowly around the square gossiping. But out of the corner of her eye she could see Fernando, with the boys, and she knew he was watching her each time she came by.

She loved going into the cool quiet of the church for early-morning Mass and seeing the serene sisters who taught her at the Catholic school. And then there were the parties they had at the boys' fraternity house! And she loved it when they all went down to the ocean to swim, sometimes at San Juan or Luquillo, and sometimes at Ponce. But what she loved almost more than anything else were the big family parties they often had on Sunday, when they would eat a roast pig, fixed with plantains, which had been started on the open fire at dawn. Her mother and aunts would make *tortillas* and *asopoa* and cook huge plates of beans, and bake fancy cakes, and they'd eat rich, juicy mangoes and thick slices of fresh pineapple. Everyone would sit around talking and laughing, until suddenly someone would start singing. Then, before you knew it, the boys had their guitars out, and they would go from one old Spanish song to another. Everyone, from the old grandparents to the tiny tots would join in, and they would all sit on until way after dark, watching the embers of the fire die out.

Most of the time she wanted none of it to change. She couldn't imagine what it would be like not to wake up to the warm sun, not to see the hedge of hibiscus around their house or the *alcalifa* or the poinsettia, and not to hear the song of the *coqui* nor to smell the sweet odor of the *almendra* outside her window as she drifted off to sleep.

She couldn't picture life's being different from what it was—seeing her friends, Maria and Pilarín, every day, going to Father Sebastian for confession, and wondering whether she would go on to the college to be a nurse, unless before that Fernando asked her to be his wife. If he did, they would live in a little house of their own on a hillside just like the one her father had built his house on, and in the spring her father would lend Fernando his pair of oxen to plow the field for their cabbages and yams.

But when Carlos started talking about New York, it turned everything upside down. She felt a fire in her heart, a great, exciting restlessness to go beyond the mountains encircling the village. How terrible it would be to live and grow old without ever seeing anything except her small island! She felt a burning urgency to go now, while she was young and free.

"Felicidad. . . ." There was her mother calling again.

"Come on, Willy." She pulled herself up. "Come and help me with the tubs. I've got to do the washing."

As they ran up to the house there was a sudden, quick rain. Felicidad liked the cool feel of it against her face, but she went about her work, knowing the rain would last only a few minutes. That's the way I am, she thought, fiery like the sun, and then cooling off, as if washed by the rain. But like the weather here, the cloudy moods never last long!

Chapter 2

Mrs. Marquez stood back and looked at her daughter admiringly. "She is the joy of my life," she said with a gay laugh. She had to stand up high and straight to adjust the fine tortoise-shell comb she was placing in the bun of dark, lustrous hair piled on top of Felicidad's head. Felicidad often teased her pretty dark-eyed mother about being shorter than she was.

"Does she bring you more joy than Carlos or me?" Willy asked teasingly. The men in the family were also admiring their Felicidad, while, in the middle of the living room, her mother was putting the finishing touches to her party attire before she left for the dance with Carlos.

"Where is your fan?" Mrs. Marquez asked. "Willy, run and get it for her. It is in my room."

"You didn't answer my question," he said insistently.

"*Pobrecito,* I feel sorry for you. I love my three children equally, but for a mother a daughter is different. You don't wear a ball gown," she added, laughing.

"I should say not!" Willy retorted indignantly, and fetched the fan for his sister.

Felicidad fluffed out her skirt nervously. It was all very well for the members of her family to admire her and to think she looked nice. But what would all her sorority sisters think? And Fernando, what would his eyes tell her?

Felicidad took the ivory fan from Willy and tried holding it every which way. It was her mother's fan, and she felt awkward and self-conscious with it. The more she felt her father's and brothers' eyes on her, the more self-conscious she became. This was her first long dancing frock, and she had made it herself, but that was not what bothered her. She knew the stitches were fine (maybe not as tiny as her mother's would be, but pretty close), and that her satin pumps with their curved French heels and pointed toes were in the height of style. Her tiny gold earrings, which had belonged to her grandmother, were family heirlooms to be proud of, and her long white gloves, which had also been her mother's, were of the finest, softest leather. Everything was right except herself.

She felt that she would never learn to walk and to sit gracefully the way her mother did, or the way Pilarín, her best friend, did. She was awkward and stupid, and Fernando would only dance with her because he felt sorry for her, and because he was a good friend of Carlos.

"Hold your fan this way." Mrs. Marquez took the fan and held it loosely and easily in her hand, opening and closing it and opening it again to show Felicidad how. Then, with a little flick of her wrist, she fanned herself gracefully. "Relax. It is so easy."

"It is easy for you," Felicidad said ruefully. She had longed so much for this night, and now that it was here she wished in a spasm of agony that it was over. Now that she was well past her fifteenth birthday (she would be sixteen very soon) and in her second year of high school, she had been invited to join the sorority. Tonight was the initial dance for the new girls, and she had asked Fernando to go with her. The boys had generously let the girls use the fraternity house for the dance, since the sorority did not have a house of its own. Actually, the boys didn't have a whole house either. It was a large room above Pancho's shoe store, but it had a nice smooth floor, which was fine for dancing.

How had she ever had the courage to ask Fernando to go! In truth, she hadn't been able to face him, but had written him a note instead, which she had passed to him hurriedly right after their class in religion, and before history had started. She had been afraid to look at his face while he read it, but finally she had had to lift her eyes, because she could feel him looking at her. His eyes were smiling when they met hers, and he nodded his head vigorously. It was hard to think about history after that. Who cared about all the generals who had conquered Puerto Rico? Now they were an independent commonwealth with their own elected governor, and she, for one, was glad she hadn't lived when all that terrible fighting had been going on!

"Felicidad, stand up straight." Her mother's brisk voice interrupted her daydreaming. "Keep your head up high."

Felicidad looked into her mother's eyes pleadingly. "What will I do if no one else asks me to dance? Do I just sit down along the wall? My dress will be all crushed from sitting!"

Her mother hugged her gently, careful not to disturb her hair. "You'll dance. Don't worry. But never sit alone. Go over and sit and talk with the chaperons if you have to. We'll be there in a little while. But I'm not worried. You'll be the prettiest girl at the dance."

"Mother, don't say that. You know it's not true. Pilarín is much prettier, and so is Margarita." She threw a teasing glance at Carlos, because Margarita was his girl.

Carlos smiled back at her serenely. "Of course. Margarita *is* the prettiest girl in Barranquitas. Everyone knows that."

"Only *you* know that," his mother teased him. "Don't be disloyal to your sister. She comes first."

"She has Fernando to tell her how pretty she is. She

doesn't need me," Carlos said, grinning broadly. "Come on, let's go. Everyone will be waiting for us."

Mr. and Mrs. Marquez and Willy went outside to watch Carlos help Felicidad up into the front of the pickup truck. Mr. Marquez used the truck for taking his banana crop in to the market every week, and although Carlos was saving all his money to buy a car, he didn't have enough yet.

"I wish we didn't have to go in this old truck," Felicidad said. She stood up until Carlos laid out a blanket for her to sit on, so she wouldn't get her dress soiled.

"I cleaned it for you," Willy said proudly. "I cleaned it as much as I could."

"Thank you, Willy." Felicidad waved good-by to her parents and to Willy as Carlos started the truck up the hill. They had to pick up Margarita and Fernando before they headed down toward the village.

Felicidad's heart was beating nervously. She turned around to watch her parents wave to her, until the truck passed a curve in the road that hid them from sight. She felt as if she were going far, far away.

It's only Fernando and Margarita, she reasoned with herself, and my own brother Carlos is with me. We're only going to the fraternity house that I pass every day on my way to school. But suddenly, even the dark profile of her brother beside her looked different. She knew instinctively he was thinking about Margarita, and it made him seem a stranger. The familiar houses they passed, the violet hills—*everything* was different. Felicidad clutched the fan tightly in her gloved hands as she held her back erect and tried to quiet her rising terror. She would never be able to dance in these shoes. She should have bought a dress and not made her own. She'd never think of anything to say to Fernando. And what would she do if no one asked her to dance? Poor Fernando! She'd die of embarrassment for him!

Margarita was quivering with excitement when she came out to the truck with Carlos. Felicidad thought she had never seen anyone look so beautiful in her life. "She is a real Spanish beauty," Felicidad's mother had said of Margarita. With her pale oval face, her aristocratic nose, her large dark eyes, and her rich black hair, which was parted smoothly in the middle and caught in a loose knot with a scarlet poinsettia at the nape of her neck, Margarita was indeed a Spanish beauty. She wore a white taffeta gown with bright scarlet flowers appliquéd around the hem line, and when she walked, her dress rustled softly.

Felicidad moved over closer to Carlos to make room for her. Margarita greeted her breathlessly. "I'm so excited!" She laughed softly. "I have news. . . ." Then she stopped abruptly, her dark eyes under her long lashes glancing swiftly over at Carlos. She drew a long breath and nervously tapped the fan in her hand.

"What is your news?" Felicidad asked, dying of curiosity.

"Perhaps I should tell Carlos first," Margarita said awkwardly. "I talk too much when I am excited."

"It's too late now. You'd better tell us," Carlos ordered.

"We're going to New York!" Margarita announced. "My father made up his mind. We had a letter from my uncle. He has found a job for my father and maybe one for me. Carlos, you must come too. Soon! Will you?" She looked across Felicidad at Carlos again, but his eyes were on the road.

"Margarita, this is exciting news!" Felicidad grasped her friend's hand warmly. "Carlos, we must go. We must!"

Carlos' profile was stern. "We shall see," was all he said, but Felicidad wished Margarita had not been so impulsive. She felt that these two should have been alone when Margarita told Carlos her news. It was an accepted fact that they were in love, and surely they must have talked of marriage. What would Carlos do now?

Carlos would certainly leave home and go to New York alone. Fear gripped her heart. With Margarita gone, there'd be no keeping him, and her parents would never let Felicidad go along.

"What about your house, your father's farm? What's going to happen to all that?" Felicidad asked.

"One of my uncles is bringing his family to live in our house, and he'll take care of Papa's farm. It's all been settled very fast. I hope I get the job. And Carlos, maybe there would be one for you too," she added eagerly. Margarita was the same age as Carlos and had graduated from high school in June.

Carlos' eyes were fixed on the road, and Felicidad's heart went out to the grim mixture of pride, hurt, and determination on his face. "I am not a child. I will come myself and find a job," he said.

Felicidad wished she could disappear and leave Margarita and Carlos alone together. She felt a sense of impending doom, a sense of life's coming to a crisis. It was like this when all the clouds gathered together to warn of one of the big storms coming from across the mountains.

She had felt this sense of premonition before when bad things had happened. She had felt it before Willy had fallen out of the tree and almost broken his neck. She had also felt it the hot afternoon her father had collapsed in the field and she had, for a reason unknown to her, walked out to be with him. She had found him face down in the grass, his machete still in his hand, and he had been gasping for breath. That was when the doctor said he had a weak heart and had put him to bed for two weeks. The doctor had called it a mild attack and said he'd be all right, but ever since then Felicidad had worried about her father, and that was one more reason to be fearful of Carlos' going away. If he went to New York, they must all go with him. It seemed such a good time now for her father to give up farming and to find something easier to do in New York.

Fernando was waiting outside his house for them, and with a little wave of greeting, he climbed into the back of the truck. It seemed to Felicidad a most unromantic way to be going to such an important dance, and she sighed with apprehension about what the rest of the evening would be like.

Many young people were already there when they arrived, and the musicians—four guitarists—were playing a *merengue*. The girls had decorated the walls beautifully with huge garlands of white and yellow flowers, and yellow and white paper streamers were crisscrossed along the ceiling. Felicidad was glad her mother had selected the palest, softest blue for her dress. She knew the color looked pretty against the yellow and white.

The older sorority sisters were the hostesses and greeted them at the door. It was Felicidad's first big dance, and she glanced around the room shyly. Everyone looked so different! The girls she saw in school every day in the school uniform—a pleated skirt and middy blouse—looked like different people. There was Josie, who always had her hair in her eyes and her blouse parting from her skirt, looking tall and smooth and very grown-up in her long pink gown and with her hair brushed neatly. And Maria and Pilarín, Louisa and Chiquita—they were almost strangers with their faces made up so artfully as they went gliding around the floor in their little heeled shoes, swaying in time to the music, and smiling at their partners. What had Pilarín done to make her eyes so huge and shining?

The grownups looked strange too, all dressed up as if they were going to church. There were plenty of parents scattered throughout the room, acting as chaperons and having a good time themselves as they danced or sat at the tables sipping their cold drinks and talking.

But Felicidad didn't have much time just to look around. Fernando was beside her, and silently, with just a little smile and a nod of his head, he put his arm around her and led her off to join the dancers.

At first she had to concentrate on the steps. This was one time she didn't want to make any mistakes! But the music was so rhythmic and Fernando was such a good leader that it wasn't long before she was able to relax and let her feet take care of themselves as she floated along in Fernando's arms.

What a marvelous, wonderful event a dance was! She had never experienced anything like it in her life, and she was sure there was nothing else quite like it in the world. Out on the dance floor in the low lights it was almost like being alone with Fernando, and just the thought of being alone with him made her blush. The idea was quite frightening; she wouldn't know what to do or to say. It was a relief to know that she didn't have to worry about that for quite a few years yet. Not until she was in college or ready to get married would her parents allow her to spend any time alone with a boy. Therefore, dancing like this was both safe and wondrously exciting. She could feel Fernando's strong arms around her and his breath against her cheek, and her heart was beating so hard that she wondered if he could hear it too as he whirled her around.

"My family is going on a picnic tomorrow. We are going to Luquillo swimming. Can you come too?" Fernando spoke as if he'd been waiting all day to ask her this question and was greatly relieved to get the words out.

"I'd love to go, if I can. I'll have to ask my parents." Felicidad glanced at him shyly, and then they both smiled. The air was magically cleared. The tension they had both been feeling suddenly left them, and Felicidad sighed happily as she rested comfortably in Fernando's arms. They didn't miss a dance. They went from the *merengue* to a cha-cha-cha, and then they danced the bolero, the mambo, and the conga.

When the music stopped, Fernando led her out to a small balcony overlooking the village and the hills beyond. It was dark now, and there was no moon. The sky was studded with bright stars and seemed the texture of black velvet. Behind them, through the open doors, they could hear the voices of their friends, and outside, the little song of the *coqui* filled the night air.

Felicidad couldn't imagine a life different from this peaceful quietness, but her heart felt uneasy as she thought about Margarita's news and about Carlos. "Have you heard that Margarita is going to New York?" she asked Fernando.

Fernando nodded his head. "Yes, I know. But she won't stay. She'll be back here very soon."

Felicidad looked at him in surprise. "Why do you say that? What makes you think so?"

"Margarita won't be happy there. You wait and see if I'm not right. I hear too many bad stories about New York. And Margarita is spoiled. She is used to being the center of attraction, while in New York she'll be nobody. She won't like that."

"You only say that, because you don't want to go away." Felicidad's eyes met Fernando's before she lowered her gaze.

"No, I never do want to go away," Fernando said. The light from the ballroom lit up his profile. In repose his face was sad, in spite of his strong nose and chin. Even now he had the resigned, slightly cynical look of so many Spanish men, as if he already knew the sorrows of the world and his own helplessness in changing them.

Felicidad couldn't remember a time when she hadn't known Fernando. When she was a little girl and they used to go down to the creek to play with the other children, Fernando had always been by her side. He was the one who would pick her up when she stumbled on the rocks, and who would proudly bring her gifts of frogs with their shiny, bulging eyes. Felicidad accepted them unblinkingly, never letting him know that later she slipped them back into the creek to hop away.

She had counted on Fernando, who was ahead of her, when she'd first gone to school. She had been proud to be so grown-up, yet shy and afraid, grateful for Sister Concepción's kind, understanding face, and terrified of Sister Maria's stern one, and always she had looked across the room for the safety of Fernando's warm smile and his soft brown eyes.

Now his eyes were not soft, and there was a hint of scorn in them. "People are fools to go up to New York. They should stay home and work in Puerto Rico. There is a lot to do here."

"Taking care of chickens and pigs! I think Carlos is right. There are jobs in New York, and you can make more money. Besides, I'd like to see it, wouldn't you?"

Fernando shrugged his shoulders. "What for? What's there to see?"

"Oh, Fernando!" Felicidad shook her head impatiently. "You never want anything to change! Don't you want to see the world? Do you always want to stick on your farm and see nothing but cabbages and bananas, and do the same thing day after day?"

"I don't mind. It was good enough for my father and for your father, so it is good enough for me. I like a quiet, peaceful life."

"Fernando, you make me so angry!" Felicidad felt as if she wanted to shake him. "You have no sense of adventure, no curiosity. You sound like an old man."

"Why do you want to go to New York so badly?" Fernando demanded angrily. "To go out with New York boys? To meet gangsters?"

"They're not all gangsters! And maybe I do want to meet New York boys. What's wrong with that? I'd like to meet someone who wants to be something more than just a farmer, someone who wants a little excitement in his life!"

"Go ahead," Fernando said stiffly. "Who's stopping you? I suppose now, with Margarita going, Carlos will go, and you too. I hope you like it."

"I wish I could go," Felicidad said. "But I'd want my parents to come along," she added.

"Perhaps they will," Fernando said, without looking at her. "But you will have to say good-by to me."

"That is your fault, not mine," said Felicidad miserably. "Besides," she added helplessly, "we probably won't go."

"The States! The States! Everybody wants to be American. We should be Puerto Rican, be ourselves. It never did us any good to belong to Spain *or* to America!" Fernando said impatiently.

"I think we're fine the way we are," Felicidad retorted. "I don't know about politics, whether we should become the fifty-first state or not, but wanting to see New York has nothing to do with the way I feel about Puerto Rico! I love it just as much as you do."

"Why do you want to fight with me on such a night as this?" Fernando's eyes were miserable as they turned to hers.

"I don't want to fight," she said stubbornly. "We just don't agree, that's all."

"Let's go back and dance. It's better to dance than to fight," Fernando said.

Felicidad took the arm he offered her, but she felt angry with herself and with him. What would her mother say if she knew she had had such an argument with Fernando? And on a night like this, her first big dance! Her mother did not believe a woman should ever argue with a man and that at all times she should be serene and calm. But that was very difficult, especially if a boy was stubborn like Fernando, and you had ideas and thoughts of your own.

The band was playing a *merengue*, and whirling to the lively music made her forget everything except the wonderful rhythm and the glorious fun of dancing. To her great surprise, Felicidad found she had plenty of dancing partners. There were Miguel, Luis, Alfonso, and Joey—boys she had always known—yet tonight they were shy strangers, dressed up and looking as if they were going to church—except for their faces, which were not solemn tonight, but gay.

She waved a greeting to Willy and her parents when they arrived, proud that she would not have to embarrass them by being a wallflower. Felicidad was pleased to see her parents join the dancing, glad that they looked so handsome on the floor and were not like some of the other chaperons who sat along the wall and gossiped and criticized.

Suddenly she remembered Fernando's invitation for the picnic tomorrow. Would he still want her to go? Later, when they said good night, he remembered too, and said he hoped she hadn't changed her mind.

"I'll ask my parents," she said demurely, and that was all. Inwardly, she was very glad that Fernando's eyes were begging her to come.

Chapter 3

The square was still, with the kind of stillness that fills the air very early on Sunday morning. It was as if nature herself knew that the seventh day, the day of rest, had arrived, and that she, too, should pause to reflect and to catch her breath for the week ahead.

The Marquez family had come to church for seven o'clock Mass, and as Felicidad knelt beside her mother, she felt repentant for her anger with Fernando, which was still smoldering within her. After all, Fernando had spoken almost word for word as her parents always did, and after a swift glance at her mother's serene face lowered in prayer, Felicidad's conscience stabbed her with remorse. She had never in her life wanted anything other than what her parents said was right. Why did she feel now, as Carlos did, such a longing to go away?

And how did she really feel about Fernando? Even now, when her mind should be dwelling on the gentle Jesus, it went dancing about, thinking of the day ahead

to be spent on the beach with Fernando. And only last
night she had wanted to shake him and had felt she
could go off, just like that, and say good-by to him.
Maybe Fernando and her father were both right.
Maybe she should be content to stay here and follow in
the tradition and the customs of the village ways . . .
and marry Fernando.

How immodest she was to think about Fernando this
way, when he hadn't as yet declared himself. She must
stop thinking about him *now!* She must think about
the Blessed Virgin and ask forgiveness for her own way-
ward thoughts and pray for guidance and understanding. The good Virgin seemed close to her here in the
soft light of the candles. The glint of the sun lighting
up the beautiful stained-glass windows, the mellowness
of the church, and the bittersweet odor of incense all
filled her with a warm, sweet comfort and a sense of
time unchanging.

The sun was bright when they came out of the dim-
ness of the church. Felicidad took off her black-lace
mantilla and folded it into her bag. Now to go home
and help her mother get ready for the picnic. It had
been decided that the two families were going together
—Fernando's family, the Riveras, and the Marquezes.
And thank goodness her father was borrowing his
brother's car, so they wouldn't have to ride in that old
truck!

At home she and her mother cooked a chicken, cut it

up, and wrapped it in waxed paper. They cut off thick slices of pork, which they fried crisp, and wrapped them also. They packed pineapple, mangoes, and oranges, and a bag of candy for the children. They also put into the food hamper long loaves of native white bread and cold bottles of soda and a thermos of their favorite drink, *café con leche*.

"Don't forget the umbrella," Mrs. Marquez reminded Felicidad.

Felicidad was gathering up bathing suits and towels for everyone. She was so excited she couldn't stand still. Willy was running around outside, chasing the dog and telling all his friends and the neighbors that they were going on a picnic. Carlos and his father were washing the borrowed car, so that it would be clean and shiny for the trip.

Soon the Rivera family was outside, honking the horn loudly for them. "Come on! Come on!" Willy came rushing in wildly. He tripped over the food hamper and fell down in such a comical way that Felicidad and her mother laughed until they both had to sit down to catch their breath.

"Laugh in the morning, cry at night," Mrs. Marquez said, wiping her eyes.

"We have nothing to cry about," Felicidad said gaily.

"I guess not," her mother agreed.

When they finally took off, their neighbors from the other houses on the hill came out to wave and wish them a good time. The dog was barking to add his own farewell, and the two cars, filled to overflowing with parents, children, and food, blew their horns in salute.

Mr. Marquez was driving, and he kept close behind the Rivera car, where Felicidad could see Fernando's head bobbing up and down. Mr. Rivera stopped short every few miles along the way to greet his various friends, and Felicidad had to brace herself from falling when her father stopped unexpectedly, which he had to do often so as not to hit Mr. Rivera's car. It was a glorious day, and everyone was outdoors, going or coming from church, or just standing in the road being sociable. They also had to make many stops to avoid hitting the goats, chickens, and dogs that were apt to be ambling along in front of the cars.

Hibiscus everywhere was scenting the air, and as they went down the narrow mountain road, it was cool and fresh, for they were shaded from the hot sun by heavy *flamboyán* trees. Willy was softly whistling a tune, and Felicidad added her voice to his. Soon they were all singing their favorite Spanish songs.

In about two and a half hours they reached the beach at Luquillo, and fortunately the huge parking lot was not overcrowded. The boys carried the hampers of food down to the beach, and the men and women parted, Felicidad going with her mother and Mrs. Rivera and the Rivera girls to the women's locker. For ten cents they each had a locker for their clothes and fine, immaculate dressing rooms to change in. Everyone was very proud of Luquillo and kept it clean and shining.

The white beach stretched out in each direction for several miles, with not a piece of paper nor speck of food to mar it. The smooth sand was spotted with groups of people, and the palm trees swayed gently and provided shade for those who wanted it. Best of all was the water, which was the bright blue of the tropics, and here in the deep curve that formed the beach were only gentle waves, instead of the rough surf found along most of the coast line.

The sun on the beach was hot, and everyone went into the water, grownups and children alike. Fernando quickly caught up with Felicidad, and they swam side by side away from the others. Felicidad turned over lazily and floated on her back. Unlike a good many children brought up in the mountains, she swam well, and Fernando, like his father, was an especially fine, strong swimmer. However, the others swam very little. Mrs. Marquez, Mrs. Rivera, and the children played near the shore, and although Felicidad's father swam a little, he, too, kept to the shallow water.

Fernando turned on his back and floated alongside Felicidad. They were both silent. This was their first moment alone since their argument the previous night. Felicidad was filled with the warm glow she had felt in church and with the clear beauty of the day. She wanted to tell Fernando she was sorry she had been so sharp with him, but she didn't know how to say it. She was afraid that if she mentioned it, they might start arguing all over again, and the day would be spoiled for them both.

"Watch out! There's a barracuda!" Fernando cried out suddenly. Felicidad jumped, and with a shriek, she thrashed the water wildly as she tried to get out of the way. Then she saw Fernando's face, and she knew he was teasing her about her constant dread of meeting a barracuda in the water.

"Oh, you!" she shouted, splashing water into Fernando's laughing face. "I'll get you!" she cried, pretending great anger and indignation, as she tried unsuccessfully to duck him. Inwardly she was relieved. This was Fernando's boyish way of making up, of saying, "Let's forget about last night. Today we are together in the sunshine. Let's not be serious. Let's enjoy ourselves and have a good time."

And today Fernando was right. How glorious life was, when she could swim with him in the cool water with a cloudless blue sky overhead and their two families close by having a gay time.

"The Puerto Ricans are a childish people," she had once heard a tight-lipped lady tourist from the continent say in the fashionable inn in Barranquitas where she occasionally went to help out. Were they childish? Was it childish to enjoy life, to want to laugh with those you love, and to play silly jokes? Was it childish for her father and Fernando not to be ambitious to make much money but to want to stay here and enjoy the sunshine, the hills, and the blue water? And Carlos, would he ever really be happy anywhere else?

Today she never wanted to leave. She wanted to stay here and someday marry Fernando and have her own children and her own house. She wanted to go on picnics and to dance with Fernando and to tell foolish little jokes, to laugh and sing songs.

They were being called, because it was time to eat. Everyone came tumbling out of the water and up into the shade of the palm trees for lunch. There were five Rivera children who were younger than Fernando. They were quiet and well-mannered and waited patiently with longing eyes for their mother to give them their food. Felicidad helped the women spread a large tablecloth over the sand and get everyone settled around it. Then they unpacked the food hampers. Everything looked and tasted even better than it did at home, and everyone ate heartily.

Soon Fernando picked up his guitar and began playing, and the others joined in the singing. Felicidad stretched out lazily on her back, but she held her head so that she could watch Fernando's face. When he sang and played this way, even in the midst of all the gaiety, there was a faraway look of sadness in his eyes that touched her to the core. This is what I love about him, she thought. He knows and he understands. He is truly everything that is Puerto Rican. This is what we are, he and I. We know how to laugh and to sing, but we also know that there is much sorrow in life.

Felicidad thought often about her classmates who lived in *las arrabales* (slums) down along the creek in Barranquitas, where there were neither roads nor sidewalks. How did they manage? Where did they do their homework at night? How did they bathe, get dressed, brush their hair until it was glossy and shining, and do up their dresses, which they starched and ironed so crisply and freshly? Their houses were like chicken houses, thin and flimsy, one on top of the other. They had no floors or windows. They were just mud shacks, with the chickens and pigs and all the children running in and out. There was no furniture inside, just a cot to sleep on and maybe an old broken-down table or chair, and close by outside were the cages, where the cocks were so lovingly cared for. If it wasn't for her father's farm and the hard work he and Carlos did, they would be living the same way. Poverty was always so close in Puerto Rico; it was what gave the people that sadness in their eyes, even when they were laughing and singing. But things were getting better, and many of the slums were disappearing, while fine new housing developments were going up. Everyone was saying Puerto Rico was on its way to prosperity.

After a while Fernando put aside his guitar and

pulled Felicidad to her feet. "Come, let's go for a walk," he said, and she willingly followed him. They walked down the beach looking for sand dollars, and then went up under the palm trees to tease the "sleepy grass." Felicidad loved to touch the grass and watch it curl up as if to go to sleep and then, after a while, see it stretch itself out and wake up again.

When they came back to join the others, Mrs. Marquez was begging Felicidad's father not to go back into the water. "You ate too much dinner," she said.

"That was a long time ago," Mr. Marquez replied. "It is nice and cool in the water." Both Felicidad and her mother followed his eyes to the water where his friend, Mr. Rivera, was swimming vigorously out to the buoy. "He swims well, doesn't he?" Mr. Marquez said. He seemed both admiring and envious, like a little boy who has been left out of things. "I'll go for a little swim too," he said, walking toward the water.

Mrs. Marquez said nothing, but she watched her husband anxiously. Felicidad knew her mother could not say the words in both their minds, words that were obvious but which would hurt Mr. Marquez's pride, "You don't swim as well as Mr. Rivera, and besides, remember your heart."

Like a great many men, especially Latin Americans, Mr. Marquez was both sensitive about his physical prowess and proud of it. He did not like to be reminded of any lack of skill and certainly not of any physical

weakness, such as that of his heart. Determinedly he
went into the water, and with unnecessarily energetic
strokes, swam out toward Mr. Rivera.

Felicidad watched her father nervously. Swim easier.
Don't work so hard, she was saying wordlessly, wishing
she could call out to him. Her mother, too, watched
silently, and involuntarily shrugged her shoulders in a
gesture of helplessness. "He's like a little boy," she
murmured.

Instinctively Felicidad walked down close to the surf
to watch the two men in the water, Mr. Rivera swimming easily and confidently close to the buoy, her
father splashing the water needlessly, halfway there.

Suddenly, even as she was watching him with her
eyes glued to his black hair, his head disappeared under
the water. His legs went down too, and when his head
reappeared some nerve-racking, breathless seconds
later, she knew he was in trouble.

"Help! Help!" she screamed. "Papa! Papa!"

She rushed into the water and started swimming toward the spot where that precious head had disappeared again. She could hear her mother screaming
from the beach, and then two swift swimmers raced
past her. Praying silently, she gratefully recognized Fernando and Carlos ahead of her. "Dear God, please let
them get to him in time."

Mr. Rivera, too, had made a dash toward her father,
and then he and the boys were all close together. Mr.

Rivera seemed to have hold of her father. It all happened so fast! Felicidad ran out of the water to the beach, where the other bathers had gathered in a quiet, tense group around Mrs. Marquez. Willy stood near them, wide-eyed and frightened. Mrs. Rivera was close beside her mother, holding her hand, and Felicidad ran to the other side of her. Her mother's eyes were closed, and she was praying. Felicidad made the sign of the Cross, and she, too, prayed silently.

Then Carlos was carrying their father out of the water, holding him in his arms like a child. Unbelievingly Felicidad heard him say a few words to Willy and watched Willy go speeding off toward the village. She knew her younger brother was going for the priest.

The crowd drew back while Mr. Rivera and Carlos tried to administer artificial respiration to the limp body of Mr. Marquez. Felicidad and her mother sat silently near him, watching and praying for a sign of life. A man came rushing from the crowd with a medical kit, saying he was a doctor. He knelt down and held his ear close to Mr. Marquez's heart, and then took out his stethoscope and held that to it. Felicidad turned away and covered her face with her hands. The doctor's face was solemn as he gently held her father's head in his lap. Mrs. Marquez was kneeling beside her husband, holding both his hands in hers.

Felicidad prayed fervently for the priest to come quickly, and then he appeared, running to them with Willy. She buried her head against her mother as the priest knelt beside her father, for she knew he was dying. When, in a few minutes, the priest beckoned to her, she bent over and tenderly kissed her father good-by.

"Tragedy is a part of our lives," Father Sebastian was saying. He was at home with them after Mr. Marquez's funeral. Mrs. Marquez was sitting upright in her chair, her heavy black veil still on. Felicidad wished her mother would cry, but she knew she wouldn't in front of them.

This was Felicidad's first close contact with tragedy and death, and she was torn between her terrible grief and her own reluctance to accept her father's death as the will of God.

"He didn't have to die," she kept saying over and over again, and both her mother and Father Sebastian gently reproached her.

"It is as God wills it," her mother said. Her own gentle face was rigid with grief, yet she kept herself magnificently composed. Felicidad drew some solace from her mother's deep religious steadfastness, and wished that she, too, had the same unfailing faith.

"You are too young yet," Father Sebastian said kindly, "to understand His wisdom fully. But comfort yourself, child, with the memory of your fine father.

He was gentle and kind and proud, and you and your brothers have a heritage to be proud of. Comfort your mother. She needs her children closer to her now than ever. You are fortunate," he said to Mrs. Marquez, "to have three fine children. Carlos can take care of the farm, and young Willy can help him."

Mrs. Marquez lifted her veil. Her face was composed, but her grief stared through her eyes, and the touch of tragedy had already changed her from the gay, laughing woman Felicidad had known.

"I'm worried about Carlos," Mrs. Marquez said. "He hates farming. Poor Carlos, this will be a terrible burden for him to bear. I don't know what to do."

The answer seemed suddenly and sharply clear to Felicidad. Now they must go away. It seemed the best thing for all of them. Everywhere she looked she was reminded of her father with a sharp pang: the empty chair by the table where he always sat, the hooks on the wall where his old straw hat and outdoor jacket were still hanging. And when she looked out over the fields, she was sure he must be coming in soon from the farthest acre. How much worse it must be for her mother, whose eyes had always shone more brightly when her father was in sight.

Yes, going away was the answer. But it was not yet time to discuss plans with her mother. Felicidad still couldn't quite believe that her father was really gone, and right now she wanted only the warmth of her mother's hand in hers, so she could gather from her mother some of the strength that was hers and give her in return all the love that was overflowing in her own heart.

Chapter 4

Felicidad was out in the field helping Carlos and Willy with the banana plants. The boys were cutting back the old plants with their machetes, and Felicidad was stacking them in piles to be burned. Carlos' face was streaked with dirt, and his eyes were tired and grim. With every stroke of his machete his distaste for what he was doing showed unmistakably. His natural grace and the clean, sharp efficiency of his movements only made it worse, for they seemed to emphasize the rebellion in his spirit. One felt as if any minute there would be a violent eruption of his emotions, belying the smooth physical control of his body.

It was several weeks since their father's tragic death, and Felicidad felt as if all four of them in the household had been holding their breath and waiting. With Margarita gone and Carlos carrying the main burden of the farm work, he was like an unruly horse tied down in the stable. At any moment he might bolt and run.

As for Felicidad herself, she was now convinced that

the only solution for them was to move up to New York. When she told this to Fernando, his answers once again provoked her to anger.

"You say it is best for your mother," he said, "but you're the one who wants to go! You want to meet New York boys and to have wild times—to do things you wouldn't dare try at home here in Barranquitas!"

"You have no right to say such things," Felicidad retorted indignantly. "Yes, I would like to meet some New York boys and girls, and if you had an ounce of gumption, you would too. You wouldn't just want to stay here with your cabbages and your pigs!"

"I like my cabbages and pigs," Fernando said. "I don't have to go chasing all over to find out what I like. I like it here, and I feel sorry for you if you don't."

"I don't need you to feel sorry for me," Felicidad said furiously. "I like it here just as much as you do, but that doesn't mean I don't want to *see* something else! But you're too . . . too"—she searched frantically for the right word—"too stuck in the mud to want to see *anything!*"

She walked off indignantly, leaving Fernando in the square with a hurt look on his face.

As for Willy, Felicidad felt he was actually terribly scared at the thought of leaving their little island, but it was the last thing in the world he would ever admit. Also, he wanted to be wherever Carlos was, so that in their private conversations Willy bravely agreed with him.

Their mother was the big problem. A few times Carlos had mentioned moving up to New York, but Mrs. Marquez had acted as if she hadn't heard him. Carlos certainly didn't disguise his hatred for farm work, and his mother would listen to him sympathetically, but again, Felicidad had the feeling that she didn't really hear him.

Her mother seemed to be moving in a quiet, sorrowful world of her own, and it frightened Felicidad. She felt as if they were drifting, with no one to guide them. The Marquez children were used to having their parents make decisions for them, but their mother either didn't want to, or else she wasn't able to make a decision. She just went on from day to day, seemingly unaware that Carlos was likely to take a drastic step at any moment.

Today, out in the field, Felicidad made up her mind to speak to Carlos. When he sat down to rest and have a smoke, she said to him, "I think you should talk to Mama about moving to New York. It's foolish to go on this way."

Carlos looked at her nervously. "Why me? Why don't you speak to her? You want to go too."

"You are the head of the house now," Felicidad said. "You must take the initiative."

"Mama's still the boss," Willy said. "Carlos isn't our father."

"Of course he's not," Felicidad said. "But he is the elder son. I think he should tell Mama that we all want to go and that we think it's the best thing for her, too."

"Why are you so anxious to go away?" Willy asked teasingly. "Did you have a fight with Fernando?"

"Fernando has nothing to do with it," Felicidad said with dignity, but she blushed in spite of herself.

"Let's all talk to Mama," Carlos suggested. "Tonight, at supper. Margarita said in her last letter that her father is sure he can get me a job. We'll rent the farm, and we'll all be better off!" His eyes shone at the prospect.

"I can work too." Willy backed up his brother. "In New York there is a pile of jobs!"

"You have to go to school," Felicidad admonished him. Her heart was quickening its beat. They could really do it! The three of them could persuade their mother.

"Margarita says New York is a wonderful place," Carlos went on eagerly. "There are lots of people, always something happening. She is crazy about it. She saw Radio City already—she went to a movie there at nine o'clock in the morning!" His eyes were bright with enthusiasm.

"We'll go up in an airplane," Willy said in awe.

"And I'll buy a dress in a Fifth Avenue store," Felicidad said, looking out across the fields. Instead of the trees and the mountains, she saw a dazzling avenue lined with beautiful shops that were filled with wonderful things.

That night, while they were sitting at the table eating their evening meal, Carlos cleared his throat and spoke to their mother. He started off nervously, but as he went on talking and adding up all the reasons for moving that he and Felicidad had discussed, his own enthusiasm took over. They would make more money, Carlos told her. He would have a future, and so would Willy. Besides, he added, the change would be good for her, and she would be near her very close friend, Margarita's mother, Mrs. Esteves. "It's the best thing for all of us," he ended up, watching his mother anxiously.

The expression on her face changed very little. She was still resigned, sad, and a little bewildered, as she had been ever since her husband's death. "It's been so long since I've traveled anywhere," she said. "I don't know. . . ."

"But Mother, Carlos hates farming so much," Felicidad pleaded. "Don't you think he should have a chance?"

Her mother smiled at her indulgently. "You're putting it all on poor Carlos. What about you, daughter? Do you really want to go?"

Felicidad nodded her head. "Margarita makes it

sound so exciting! I'm dying to see New York for myself."

"And you, Willy?" His mother turned to him.

"I may get to be a millionaire in New York," Willy said, and his droll face made them all laugh.

"If your father were alive, it would be different," Mrs. Marquez said quietly. "But if this is what you all want, I won't stand in your way."

Carlos picked up his mother in his strong arms and hugged her, twirling her around gaily. "You won't be sorry. You'll be happier. I promise you," he said.

Mrs. Marquez sighed. "I don't look for much happiness any more. Just pleasure from you, my children. Carlos, you make me dizzy!"

After supper they sat around the table making plans. There was so much to be done! The farm had to be disposed of and arrangements made with Margarita's family in New York for a place to live. Carlos needed a job, and there was packing to do. Money for the fare had to be saved up. . . .

Soon Carlos and Willy rushed out to tell the news to all their friends. Felicidad sat outside with her mother, her head dizzy. New York City! From looking at the magazines that came from the States, she knew the names of some of the streets, such as Broadway and Fifth Avenue. In the pictures it all looked splendid. She could imagine herself looking like the girls in the pictures, in a ball gown, or walking on Fifth Avenue and peering into all the fine shops.

But as she looked out over the hills she thought of Fernando, and she was filled with misgivings. Did she really want to say good-by to him? It was his own fault, though. He could go to New York too, if he wanted to. But no! He was just a farmer, and that was all he ever wanted to be!

What would it be like in a strange city, so far away from home? And what about her English? They all studied it in school, but none of them could really speak it. She could read English a little, but to have to use it to get along. . . . Well, other Puerto Ricans managed, so they would too.

The next few weeks flew by in a whirl of excitement for the Marquez family. Disposing of the farm was no problem. With so many uncles, aunts, and cousins in the family, there was always some member of it who needed a home or a job or both. This time it was one of Mr. Marquez's nephews, who was married and had three small children. His seasonal job, cutting sugar cane, was over, and he and his wife were only too happy to move to their late uncle's farm and run it for as long as they could have it.

So the young Castillo family moved in, which naturally added to the general confusion. The next problem was waiting to hear from Margarita about a job for Carlos, and the third, and most important, was how to get the money for the fare.

Carlos had the money he had been saving for an automobile, but that wasn't enough to buy plane tickets for all of them, and since Mr. Marquez had never made enough to be able to save, that was all the cash they had. After a lot of discussion, as well as resistance from Mrs. Marquez, it was decided that Carlos should go up to New York first and the others would follow.

This solution made Felicidad very uneasy. Like her mother, she hated the idea of the family's being separated. She was afraid that Carlos would be in New York and that she, Willy, and her mother would be stuck at home. Now that they had made the decision to go, Felicidad couldn't wait to take off.

As she said to Pilarín one afternoon, as the two girls walked arm in arm around the plaza, "All I think about is going. But I hate leaving you." She squeezed Pilarín's arm affectionately. "Margarita says it is so exciting! She went dancing until three o'clock in the morning, all alone with a *puertorriqueño*. They were all by themselves! Can you imagine!"

Pilarín's face was shocked. "I'd be scared. Did she write that to Carlos? What did he say?"

Felicidad laughed. "No, she didn't say that to Carlos —she wrote it to Louisa. Carlos would have had a fit. He is too strict anyway."

"Are you going to do things like that when you live in New York? I wonder what it will be like!"

Felicidad's eyes had a shining, faraway look. "I think it must be wonderful. I wish you were coming with us."

"But what about Fernando? Won't you be sad at leaving him?" Pilarín shot a glance across the square at Fernando, who was sitting and talking with a group of boys. Each time the girls walked past them, the boys would make some teasing remarks. The girls would giggle and go on their way without stopping, but invariably, they would slow down their steps as they approached the boys once again.

Felicidad blushed. "What is there to leave?" she asked, shrugging her shoulders. "I am nothing to him."

Pilarín laughed at her friend's nonchalance. "You know better than that. He keeps looking at you all the time, and I noticed you were with him most of the time at the sorority dance."

"Well, I suppose if he really cared for me he wouldn't want to stay here and just be a farmer! If he wanted to, he would come to New York too." Felicidad tossed her head defiantly, although she knew very well that her heart beat faster each time they passed Fernando and each time his eyes, lazy and seemingly half-closed under his thick, curly lashes, pierced her with their glance.

"Maybe," Pilarín said gently, "he thinks that if you really cared for him, you would stay here and in a couple of years, when you graduated, you would be content to be a farmer's wife."

Felicidad's face paled. "But my brother wants to go," she said. "Besides, there's no future in this village. I don't want to take care of pigs and chickens all my life. No thank you!" Her voice became firm, but in spite of the bravado with which she spoke, she felt her heart tremble at the thought of saying good-by to so much that she knew and loved.

It was a hot, sunny day in October when Carlos finally took off. It seemed as if all of Barranquitas was at the airport to see him go. His friends from the fraternity came, a good many of Margarita's relatives—all of them sending special messages to their cousins, aunts, and uncles in New York—and of course, the entire Marquez clan. They ranged from infants in their mothers' arms, to Felicidad's paternal grandmother, a tiny, wiry woman with a stern face and large, bright eyes, who carried her umbrella with her wherever she went and did not step across a street in the sunshine without opening it. Now she was sitting very erectly on one of the benches in the waiting room, dressed in her habitual black and alertly watching everything that went on. As each member of the family arrived, they came to greet her first, and she accepted their respects like a queen holding court. She was, in truth, the ruling monarch of the family.

She had a word of inquiry for everyone. How was baby Miguel's teething? Was young Alfonso getting proper grades in school? Had Luis fixed his leaking roof yet? She was a mother to them all, a dowager queen, the heart and core of the family, who was familiar with everyone's problems. Her approval and disapproval showed on her face, but she gave spoken advice only when asked for it.

Now Abuelita's disapproval showed clearly when two women and a young girl from the States sat down near her and all three of them lit up cigarettes. Her face was shocked. Puerto Rican ladies did not smoke in public.

Felicidad had to smile to herself as she watched her grandmother's face. She looked horrified, as if she longed to pray for the redemption of those women's souls. Felicidad wondered what she would say if she heard that Margarita was going about New York unchaperoned at night! It would undoubtedly be the same thing Father Sebastian said so frequently, "Our younger generation is being corrupted by other people's ways."

Yet "other people's ways" was one of the things she was so curious about. Carlos already had a look about him that was different, an eager, excited expression on his face that tore at Felicidad's heart. She wanted desperately to be going with him, and also she was afraid. Could anything possibly be so wonderful that it could come up to the expectation on Carlos' face?

Finally Carlos was in the plane, and the large, noisy machine took off. Felicidad felt as if her heart were soaring with it. She waved and waved, even when the plane was only a small speck in the sky, and she wondered how she could bear the suspense of waiting until she, too, would fly through the air to *Nueva York!*

The next few weeks sped by for Felicidad, her mother, and Willy. The letters from Carlos were brief, scrawled lines, saying that he was fine and that New York was wonderful. The important thing was that he had a job as a bus boy in the same hotel as Margarita's father and was sending money home. Every time a letter arrived, Felicidad counted up the money eagerly. Soon, soon there would be enough for the fares for the three of them.

Then came the day when Felicidad and her mother counted out two hundred and fifty dollars, and Mrs. Marquez uneasily agreed that they could go. This would pay their fare, and there would be some left over for rent and food. Carlos wasn't earning enough to take care of them, but Felicidad expected to get a job.

"Your father wanted so much for you to finish high school," Mrs. Marquez said sadly. "He wanted you to have a fine education, to go on to college."

"I've learned enough," Felicidad said lightly. "I'd rather go to work."

"You won't find it so easy working all day," her mother said. The troubled look on her face made Felicidad hug her affectionately.

"It's going to be wonderful being in New York." Felicidad wanted to cheer her mother up. "And think! In a few days we'll see Carlos and Margarita!"

"But you won't be seeing Fernando," her mother said teasingly.

Felicidad blushed. "I'll get along." Yet her heart took a plunge at the thought of saying good-by to Fernando.

The day and the night before they were to leave, the house was in a bedlam. Besides the Castillos and their three children, who were already living with them, all their other relatives and friends came to visit and to say good-by.

Felicidad was so excited that she didn't know what she was doing. She let a pot of water boil away on the stove until the smell of the scorched pan sent her mother hurrying to the kitchen. She packed Willy's one suit and only pair of shoes, which were all he had to wear on the plane, and so the bag had to be unpacked and done all over again.

"I'm so jealous," Pilarín sighed. "I wish I were going too."

"So do I. Maybe you'll come up. Maybe we could get jobs together."

"I have to finish school first. But I don't think my parents would let me anyway." Pilarín had brought Felicidad a beautiful string of dark-red beads. Felicidad put them on immediately, and they looked lovely against her skin.

Everyone arrived, bringing presents, and Felicidad and her mother wondered where they would pack everything. And of course all the guests had to be fed. Happily, the kitchen had been taken over by Mrs. Castillo and Mrs. Marquez's sisters, and they shooed Mrs. Marquez and Felicidad out. "Go away. We do the work today," they said good-naturedly. And indeed they did. Marvelous plates of *arroz con pollo, plátano frito,* and *habichuelas* kept appearing, along with ice-cold soda.

Felicidad thought it was a lovely party. Everyone was very gay. Yet underneath was a note of sadness at the thought of saying good-by to so many dear ones, and somehow it seemed like a final, tearing good-by to her father. This was his home and the place he had loved, where they had all lived together for as long as she could remember. Felicidad felt apprehensive and unhappy, as if they were deserting their father by leaving home and going so far away.

In the dusk of the afternoon she stole away with her mother to the hillside cemetery where her father was buried. They tended the flowers, which Mrs. Castillo had promised to take care of, and left a large, fresh wreath. Together they knelt silently and prayed. Kneeling beside her own mother, Felicidad felt very close to the Little Child, to St. Joseph, and to the Blessed Mother. A fresh breeze blew down from the mountain, rustling the leaves of the mango trees and fluttering through the scarves tied around their heads. It was a quiet and love-filled moment that she was to think of often in the tumultuous months ahead.

When they returned home, Felicidad was happy to see that Fernando and his family had arrived. She had been watching out for him all afternoon and had been worried that he might not come. Fernando looked exceptionally handsome in a bright striped sport shirt and white duck pants. He was tanned from working in the sun, and his dark hair looked blacker and his teeth whiter than ever. Felicidad wondered with a sinking heart if they'd have a chance to be alone at all, with so many people about, and she hoped fervently that Fernando would manage somehow. He did.

While the others were sitting about, singing to the guitar music, he motioned to Felicidad to slip outside. It was a glorious evening, the air was soft and fragrant, and the sky glowing with stars. Never before had the mountains looked so beautiful to Felicidad.

They walked out side by side and stood silently looking over the hills. Felicidad trembled as Fernando's hand touched hers.

"We may never see each other again," he said solemnly, his voice very low.

Felicidad shivered. "Of course we will! Won't you ever come up to New York? Why are you so stubborn, Fernando?"

He smiled at her, but his eyes were glum. "I could say the same to you. But let us not quarrel tonight, please. But why must you go?" he asked suddenly, taking her hand in his. "I can understand it for Carlos—he has Margarita there. But why you? You could stay home and live with the Castillos." His eyes were searching her face eagerly.

"But I want to go," Felicidad said simply. "I want to see what it is like. It's not so far away any more. I'll be back."

"So much can happen up there," Fernando said unhappily.

"That is what I want to find out," Felicidad said. Then she added impulsively, "I'll miss you, Fernando."

"You'll forget about me." Fernando turned his head away from her. "I'm just a dumb farmer," he said gloomily. "You'll meet all those grand New York boys!"

"I'll write and tell you about them," she said teasingly, but her heart felt heavy. She would miss Fernando terribly, and yet the excitement of going was strong within her.

Fernando scowled unhappily. Then he drew her to

him and kissed her swiftly on the mouth. "I'll never forget you, Felicidad, never! You understand?"

"I understand." With her heart racing wildly, she ran away from him and back into the house.

Chapter 5

❧❀❧

Everyone was at the San Juan airport to see them off, the same as for Carlos. Abuelita's face looked sterner than ever, but she gave her emotions away each time her eyes fell on Felicidad or her mother. They became brighter and wider, as if reaching out to hold these two precious persons forever within their gaze.

"You'll come up and visit us," Felicidad said reassuringly, patting her grandmother's tiny hand.

Abuelita smiled, but she waved her hand toward the huge plane out on the runway. "No, no. *Yo estoy aqui,*" she said. "Go with God," she added, kissing Felicidad. *"Buena suerte."*

There was so much excitement, kissing everyone good-by and having last-minute conversations, that Felicidad didn't have time to worry about actually getting into the plane and leaving the ground. The whole airport was in a hubbub, with Puerto Rican families saying good-by to their loved ones. It gave Felicidad a comforting sense of security to see so many others leaving for New York too. It made her feel less as if she were leaving her own people and everything familiar behind her.

Fernando was placing a huge box of candy in her arms. "Think of me when you eat these," he said with a grin, but his eyes were grave. He looked at Felicidad steadily, until she blushed and lowered her own eyes.

"I'll think of you even after the chocolates are gone," she said. For a wild, frantic moment she wanted to run to Abuelita and bury her head in her lap and say, "I'll stay here with you. Mama and Willy can go, but I don't want to leave."

If she closed her eyes she could still feel the sweet taste of Fernando's lips on hers last night. It had been her first real kiss, and the wonder of it stayed with her, warm and private, like the little cross she wore on a thin chain around her neck.

She stood still, feeling the loud beating of her heart. "Passengers for plane number ninety-one go to Gate Six," a voice boomed through the loud-speaker. Her heart jumped even more fiercely.

"Felicidad! Felicidad!" her mother was calling frantically. "Felicidad, we must go."

"Good-by, Fernando. I'll write to you. Will you write back?"

"Of course I will." He held her hand tightly in his, and then she turned and ran to join her mother and Willy.

Everyone had to be kissed all over again. The uncles and aunts were saying, "Maybe we'll see you in *Neuva York.*"

Felicidad's heart was racing as, with her mother in front and Willy behind, she walked up the ramp to the plane, the hot sun beating warmly on her back. Willy's eyes were almost popping out of his head. All the way over during the automobile ride into San Juan he had kept up a running conversation, full of bravado, about going up into the sky and about the questions he would ask the pilot and the navigator. But ever since he'd arrived in the large, busy, noisy airport, where he could hear the loud whir of the huge engines outside, he had clamped his mouth shut and hardly spoken a word. He had seemed to be all eyes as he watched the planes take off and looked at the people, and now that he was truly about to get on a plane himself, Felicidad thought he might burst with nervous excitement.

"Are you all right?" she whispered to him, her own stomach turning over with excitement.

Willy nodded his head. "Sure, I'm fine," he said. But Felicidad thought he looked awfully pale.

The noise of the huge engines was deafening. Then suddenly they were moving, skimming along the ground, and Felicidad held her mother's hand tightly in her own. Her stomach felt as if it were dropping out from under her as the plane left the ground. It was the oddest sensation she'd ever felt in her life, and she sat tense and rigid in her seat, her belt fastened around her, afraid to look out of the window. She wondered if she would live through the six hours it would take them to get to New York.

"Look, look!" Willy had forgotten his fears and was pulling her excitedly to the window. "Look at Puerto Rico! It's so *tiny!*" Willy said incredulously. "It's just a little speck, that's all!" His face was absolutely awe-struck, as he kept staring at the vanishing dot in the ocean that was the island on which he'd lived all his life.

Felicidad's curiosity got the better of her, and she gave in as Willy pulled her toward the window. When she looked out, she thought she'd never seen anything so beautiful before. One minute, down below was a vast expanse of blue water, into which Puerto Rico had completely vanished, and then it seemed as if they were skimming on top of mounds of whipped cream, as some soft, white, fluffy clouds floated beneath them. All her fear left her, and she settled down to enjoy the trip. She was so busy looking outside and turning about to examine the other passengers in the plane that the time sped by quickly.

There were several other children aboard, but all of them were younger than Felicidad or Willy. One mother had a baby in her arms and three small children who wanted attention. Felicidad willingly helped amuse the three little girls, while their mother took care of the baby. She read to them aloud from a book in English, so that she could practice her own English and also try to teach the children a few words. *El gato,* the cat; *la rata,* the rat—they were all such funny words that Felicidad was sure she would never have to use any of them in talking to people in New York.

It was dark by the time they approached New York, and all that could be seen were lights. There seemed to be hundreds of millions of them.

"Fasten your seat belts," the stewardess called out, and she went around helping everyone get ready for the landing.

"We're really going to be in New York!" Felicidad found herself grinning at everyone, but she didn't care whether she was being silly or not—this was the most exciting moment of her life.

The plane circled around the field, and then Felicidad felt her stomach dropping with it as it swooped down like an enormous bird and hit the ground with barely a jolt. And finally the ramp was down, the door was opened, and everyone began streaming out.

Felicidad, her mother, and Willy were at the very end of the line going out, and ahead of her, Felicidad heard cries of excitement from everyone. "Snow . . . *nieve, nieve, nieve! Tengo frío!*"

"Oh, we will freeze!" Mrs. Marquez pulled her thin coat around her as they left the warmth of the plane and stepped outside. A blast of wind blew their skirts, and Felicidad became terrified.

"*Tengo frío!* Let's go home, Mama. It's too cold!" Felicidad's eyes were running with tears from the biting air. She had not imagined anything like this, because she had never experienced anything like it before in her life. The wind and the cold were terrifying, and yet, as she watched the soft white flakes fall and rapidly cover everything in sight, the scene was also magnificently beautiful.

Excitedly Willy scooped up a handful of the snow and held it to his face. "Oh, it's cold!" he shuddered.

The woman with the baby and small children was nearby, and tears were streaming down her face. "It's *too* cold," she kept saying over and over again.

Most of the Puerto Ricans coming out of the plane were not dressed for such cold weather. Some had on thin jackets, or the women wore their shawls. Felicidad had a sweater on over her dress, but even the coat she had in her suitcase wouldn't have helped much, because it was so thin. Margarita had written to tell her to buy a warm coat at home, but Felicidad had insisted that she wanted to wait and buy one in New York.

And now the cold was so sudden, so strange and overwhelming, that all any of them could think of was to get away from the plane quickly and inside the airport. Willy and Felicidad ran, carrying their things with them, and Mrs. Marquez followed as fast as she could.

Once inside the door, everyone breathed a sigh of relief. Felicidad thought all New York had come to meet the plane, for there were many people milling about. But a lot of them were Puerto Ricans who had come to meet the new arrivals.

Where was Carlos? She looked about in frightened bewilderment. What if he didn't come! No, there he was, striding toward them. For a second Felicidad wondered if it really was Carlos, he looked so different! He had a cap jauntily set on the side of his head, a black leather jacket, and very fancy suède shoes. The jacket made him look bigger than he really was, broader and heavier, and even his hair was different, with sideburns coming down below his ears.

Carlos took them all in his arms excitedly and spoke to them rapidly in Spanish. It was so wonderful to see them, he said, and they'd have to buy some warm clothes. And how was the trip? Was it bumpy? Were they hungry? It all came in one breath!

And here were Margarita and her mother and father —everyone had come out to meet them! There was much kissing and hugging, and Carlos flew about excitedly collecting their luggage. Then he was leading them outside, and they all piled into a taxicab—all except Margarita's father and Willy, because there wasn't any more room. They were left on the sidewalk with all the suitcases. Everyone laughed, because Willy looked so forlorn, and then it was decided that he would follow with Mr. Esteves and the suitcases in another taxi.

"He won't get lost, will he?" Mrs. Marquez asked anxiously. "Can't we make room for him here?"

"No more room in this cab," the driver said impatiently. "Where do you want to go?" He spoke in English, and Felicidad could hardly understand a word he said.

Carlos gave him the address, and assured his mother that Mr. Esteves would be able to find his way home and that Willy would be perfectly safe with him. Mrs. Marquez's eyes, however, anxiously followed Willy as he disappeared into another taxi with Mr. Esteves.

Now that they were all settled in the cab, with Mrs. Esteves, Felicidad, and her mother in the back and Carlos and Margarita on the pull-out seats, there was so much to talk about that no one knew where to begin. They all looked at each other and smiled, until Mrs. Marquez started asking Carlos all the things that were on her mind. How was he getting along? How was his job? How much money had he saved? Where did he buy all the new clothes he was wearing? Hadn't they cost him a lot of money?

Carlos grinned at all her questions, but he tried to answer them as best he could. . . . Yes, he was working at the same hotel as Mr. Esteves. He was a bus boy. . . . Oh, he did everything—he set tables and cleared them and helped in the kitchen. It was a fine job. . . . Well, he hadn't been able to save much money; after all, he had sent money home for their fare, and there were so many things he needed.

Margarita teased him, saying, "He just wants to make a hit with the girls. That's why he spends all his money on clothes!"

Felicidad could hear them talking, but she really wasn't listening. Her eyes were glued to the windows as they rode over bridges and through a long tunnel. She saw lights in hundreds of windows, and people walking on the streets bundled up in heavy coats but not seeming to pay any attention to the cold or the snow at all. But here the snow wasn't as pretty as it had been. When it hit the sidewalks it was just wet like rain, and Felicidad wished she had been able to take some of that lovely white fluffy snow with her and save it.

She kept trying to imagine what it was going to be like living up here in New York City, with so many people around and so many strangers and a strange language. Then she felt a pang of lonesomeness as she thought of Fernando and of how, just last night, they were standing outside her house in the warm evening looking out over the mountains. If she closed her eyes, she could smell the hibiscus and feel the warm evening breeze in her face. She could remember exactly what his swift kiss had felt like. . . . And she blushed, thinking how much she wished she could kiss him again.

Finally the taxi stopped in front of a house that was one of a row; Felicidad wondered how anybody could tell one from the other. However, Carlos and Margarita went directly to one of the doorways and seemed to know, without any trouble, where they were going. Carlos opened the front door with a key he had on a bright gold chain.

They followed him into a dimly lit hallway, and the first thing that hit Felicidad was the very unpleasant odor. It was a vaguely familiar smell, that she didn't like, but she couldn't place it. It was her mother who said immediately, "Old cooking oil. Why don't they throw it out?"

"They can't afford to," Carlos told her. "Oil costs money."

"I thought everyone up here was so rich," Mrs. Marquez said, her eyes taking in the faded, torn wallpaper in the hallway and one large round hole, where the plaster, as well as the paper, was gone.

Both Felicidad and her mother were quiet as they followed Carlos and the others up two long flights of stairs, so dark that Felicidad was afraid she would trip and fall.

Carlos stopped in front of a door and took another key from his gold chain to open it. "Here we are," he said. "Welcome home."

They walked into a kitchen that Mrs. Esteves had

tried to make as gay as possible. At the windows she had bright striped curtains that almost hid the cardboard behind them.

"That helps keep out the wind," Carlos explained. Mrs. Esteves had decorated the wall with a large, square, gaily printed cotton, which Felicidad later discovered hid many gaping holes behind it. And right over the kitchen table was a bright Catholic image, with the words, *Dios Bendiga Nuestro Hogar* (God Bless Our Home), on it.

"This is where we live," Mrs. Esteves said of the kitchen. "We get all the water we need—good drinking water—and most of the time we get hot water." She turned on the tap to show them how hot it was.

The kitchen had a kerosene stove in the middle of it, and Carlos now turned it up to give them some warmth. "You have to be careful with this stove. I'll show you how to take care of it," he said.

"Where do we sleep?" Mrs. Marquez said. "I wonder where Willy is. I'm afraid they'll get lost."

"Don't worry. He's all right. They'll be along in a few minutes." And sure enough, at that moment a loud buzzer sounded through the apartment and made both Mrs. Marquez and Felicidad jump. Carlos pushed a button on the kitchen wall. "That must be Willy and Mr. Esteves now. I'll run down and help them with the bags." Felicidad thought it remarkable that you could press a button way up here in their kitchen and open a door downstairs.

Mrs. Esteves and Margarita showed Felicidad and her mother a small bedroom they would share with Margarita. Willy would room with Carlos, and next to the kitchen there was a small room for Mr. and Mrs. Esteves.

"All three of us are going to sleep in here?" Mrs. Marquez laughed. "It is like the doghouse we have at home—about the same size."

"Rents here are expensive," Margarita said. "We're lucky to have this. It's not too far from the subway that takes us to work." She shrugged her shoulders. "It's just for sleeping. I'm gone all day anyway, and Felicidad will probably get a job too."

"I hope so," Felicidad said eagerly. She didn't mind sharing a room with Margarita and her mother. It would be less lonesome than being all alone. "I think the room is fine," she said shyly. She wanted her mother to be happy here, and she could tell by her face that this was all very different from what she had expected.

But when Willy came upstairs, her mother's face brightened, and soon she was in the kitchen jabbering away with Mrs. Esteves. Laughing and joking, the two women got busy and prepared some food.

Mrs. Esteves was a small woman and very pretty, with heavy black hair fastened in a bun at the back of her head. She wore gold earrings that jangled when she bobbed her head around, as she did, vivaciously, when she talked. There were bracelets on her arms that tinkled when she moved. Felicidad felt it was going to be fun living here. She liked people and excitement and gaiety, and being with Margarita would be like having a sister.

There was a small portable radio on the kitchen table, and Carlos tuned in to a Spanish-speaking station. It sounded wonderful to Felicidad to hear the Spanish voices and the Spanish music.

"How is your English?" Mrs. Marquez asked Carlos, speaking, of course, in her native Spanish.

"Fine, fine," Carlos answered her in English, but then he, too, quickly reverted to Spanish. "I try to practice a little bit," he explained. "But up at the hotel they laugh at what I say, so I stick to my Spanish."

"Let them laugh. You learn English," Mrs. Marquez admonished him. "Willy, come over here to the stove. You look frozen stiff."

Willy shivered. "I'm going to get a coat like Carlos' tomorrow. It's too cold."

Mrs. Marquez sighed. "We'll all have to get some warm coats, I guess. It *is* cold here."

"I'll take you to a wonderful store on Fourteenth Street, where you can get good bargains," Mrs. Esteves promised. "Tomorrow we'll go."

They all sat around the kitchen table and drank *café*

con leche and ate bread and butter and cookies. Felicidad tried hard to keep her eyes open and to listen to the conversation, but her head began nodding. "You'd better go to bed," her mother suggested, and Felicidad agreed readily. She just about got her clothes off before she fell into the double bed she would share with Margarita, and she stayed awake barely long enough to say her prayers. She wanted to think about Fernando and about her first night in New York, but the minute her head hit the pillow she fell sound asleep.

Once during the night she awoke, startled, and sat up in bed in fright, wondering where she was. Everything was strange, and there was a bright light shining into her window. Then Margarita turned in her sleep, and Felicidad remembered. Shivering, she got out of bed and crept to the window to look outside.

The light was coming from a shaftway in a building across the courtyard. There were buildings all around, and clothes on a line, stiff with the cold. Felicidad smiled to herself at how funny the long underwear looked, hanging so stiffly. Somehow it made her feel better just seeing all those clothes. There were girls' petticoats and boys' trousers. People must be sleeping in all those buildings, and maybe some of them were Puerto Ricans too.

It was too cold to stay there long, and in a few minutes she slipped back into bed and snuggled against Margarita's warm back.

Chapter 6

When Felicidad awoke the next morning, she felt so cold she didn't think she could ever get out of bed. Her feet were like ice, and if she moved them even an inch from the one tiny spot where they were curled up, the sheet was so cold she started shaking all over. Margarita and her mother must have got up while she was still asleep, for there was no sign of them. However, she could hear voices in the kitchen, and the wonderful smell of fresh coffee drifted in to her. She must get out of bed!

She had no idea what time it was. The room was so dark and gray it could be very early in the morning—or maybe it was raining out. If only it wasn't so cold!

Her teeth were chattering as she pulled the blanket around her and gingerly put one foot and then the other on the cold floor. With the blanket wrapped tightly around her, she flew into the warm kitchen.

"You look frozen," Mrs. Esteves said, laughing.

Felicidad was astonished to discover it was almost

twelve o'clock. She went to the kitchen window and peered out. She looked out on a drab courtyard, where the backs of houses and some stray cats stared back at her, but a shaft of sunlight came filtering through.

"I thought it was raining out, it was so dark," Felicidad said in amazement. "But it's sunny!"

"It's a beautiful day," Mrs. Esteves said. "Not that you'd know it from this rat hole! Hurry up and get dressed, and we'll go shopping."

"Where is Willy?" Felicidad asked her mother. "And everyone else?"

"Carlos and Margarita left for work—they have to be there by noon. Mr. Esteves left long ago, and Willy went downstairs."

"All by himself?" Felicidad was amazed at his courage.

"Mrs. Esteves said he'd be all right now. All the children are in school anyway. He promised me he'd stay right in front of the house."

"He'll be fine," Mrs. Esteves said reassuringly. "He may as well learn right at the beginning how to take care of himself."

"He's going to have to go to school, Mama," Felicidad said. She turned to Mrs. Esteves. "Is there a school near here?"

"Of course. Lots of schools. But let him take his time. Let him learn a little English first."

"He can read some English," Felicidad said proudly.

"The kids, they learn fast. It's us older people who have a hard time," Mrs. Esteves said.

"Don't you speak any English yet?" Felicidad asked in surprise.

Mrs. Esteves shrugged her shoulders. "I can understand a little, but I get ashamed to speak. I shop in a Spanish *bodega,* and we always speak Spanish here at home, so I don't have much chance to practice. But I get along."

Mrs. Marquez gave Felicidad a heaping bowl of cereal and a cup of steaming hot *café con leche.* By their very presence, both she and Mrs. Esteves brightened up the drab, dark kitchen. Like many Puerto Rican women, they took great pride in the way they looked. They had an excellent sense of color and style, not only in wearing becoming, attractive clothes, but in the way they used cosmetics and in the care of their hair. Mrs. Esteves was wearing a dark-red woolen dress, which suited her small figure and dark coloring to perfection. Her thick hair had a brushed, gleaming sheen, and even now, in her own kitchen in the morning, her eyes were enhanced with a thin line of eye shadow. Her lipstick was carefully applied, her gold jewelry jingled, and she looked ready to meet anyone or to go anywhere.

Mrs. Marquez was more conservative in her taste and favored black, as many Spanish women do. Since she didn't own anything like a wool dress, she was wearing a simple black cotton, with a rope of pearls around her throat, and pearl earrings.

"You don't look as though you belong here," Felicidad said, eying them both thoughtfully.

"What do you mean?" her mother asked her.

"Well. . . ." Felicidad stopped short. She didn't want to hurt Mrs. Esteves' feelings, but she wondered why they were living in such a dark, dingy place. She remembered the Esteves' home in Barranquitas. She had thought their house was one of the prettiest she'd ever seen. It was painted pink on the outside, with lots and lots of flowers around it, and inside it was filled with sunlight and bright colors and looked just like Mrs. Esteves herself—trim, neat, and gay.

"I know what she means," Mrs. Esteves said. "She means this apartment. I tried to fix it up when we first moved in—we even bought some paint for the kitchen. But what's the use? It's too big a job to plaster the whole place first, and the landlord won't do anything about it. The neighbors complain that the Puerto Ricans throw their garbage out on the streets. I can understand how a woman might do that when she gets discouraged. After a while she just doesn't care. But I'm talking too much! This is your first day here. Why should I be telling you all these things?"

Mrs. Marquez looked troubled. "I hope we were wise to come up here. I miss my house already."

"You'll get used to it. Besides, there's money to make up here. My husband has a good job—he makes sixty-five dollars a week. He doesn't bring that much home, but there are no jobs like that in Barranquitas. . . . Felicidad, get dressed, and we'll go out. I'll show you some beautiful stores." Nothing seemed to bother Mrs. Esteves or to dampen her bright good spirits.

Felicidad was embarrassed, because the bathroom they used was out in the hall. They shared it with two other apartments on the floor, and she didn't want to go out wrapped up in a blanket. Understandingly, Mrs. Esteves handed her her own warm bathrobe. Felicidad put it on gratefully and decided that this was the first thing she was going to buy. She'd never owned a bathrobe in her life, and the soft warmth felt wonderful as she wrapped it around herself. She'd like to buy a nice bright-red one.

When Felicidad was dressed, her mother asked her to run downstairs, find Willy, and bring him up to get washed before they went out. Timidly, but with a sense of excitement tingling through her blood, Felicidad ran down the steps. She wished she knew who else was living in this house. She could hear voices behind the doors and walls, all of them Puerto Rican voices, speaking in Spanish.

Where were the New Yorkers? Where did *they* live?

When she stepped out on the street, both the bright

glare of the winter sun and the sudden cold made her stop short. In the apartment it had looked almost like nighttime, and the brightness of the day came as a shock. Her eyes had to get used to it. And all the strange noises she had heard only faintly from the back of the house, where their apartment was, now sounded close and very loud. Horns tooting, the backfiring of exhaust pipes on trucks, children crying and playing—the millions of noises on a crowded, congested city street—all seemed suddenly to have been turned on for her benefit, saying, "Listen. Listen. This is New York. Can you hear me?"

Felicidad pulled her sweater close and hugged herself, trying to stave off the cold wind that seemed to be wrapping itself around her and blowing through her. The worst of it was, there was no Willy standing in front of the house waiting.

How could he be standing here? she thought irritably. He'd be frozen to death by now! But her heart was pumping with a wild panic. *Where was he?* And what should she do? She was afraid to move away from the house, and she didn't want to run upstairs and tell her mother Willy had disappeared.

A young Puerto Rican woman came by pushing a baby carriage, so filled with brown bags of groceries she could hardly see the baby in it. Nervously Felicidad spoke to her in Spanish. "Have you seen a young boy around—about twelve years old, skinny, and not too tall?"

The young woman shrugged her shoulders. "I've just come from shopping. But maybe that's him fighting down the street."

"Fighting!" Felicidad looked anxiously in the direction the woman was pointing and saw two boys down on the sidewalk, pommeling each other for all they were worth.

"*Ave Maria!*" Horrified, Felicidad tore over to them, and in an excited voice she screamed at Willy to stop. She grabbed his shirt and felt like crying when a piece of it was left torn and ragged in her hand. "Stop, stop!"

Now the tears were streaming down her cheeks, both from the cold and from her fear and anger. How could Willy do such a thing! And where had he found someone to fight with? Willy wasn't a fighter—he'd get killed!

"What's the matter, lady? These kids bothering you?" Felicidad jumped at the sound of a male voice behind her, and she whirled around to face a tall man in a blue uniform.

She hadn't understood what he'd said, but his face looked kind, and she started talking to him rapidly in Spanish.

"*No comprendo* ... I don't understand," he said, but he pulled the two boys apart and stood them up on their feet. Willy was a mess. His nose was bleeding, his shirt was torn, and he still looked angry enough to start fighting again any minute.

Now Felicidad was able to get a good look at his opponent, a very handsome blond boy, just about Willy's age, but taller and stronger. Why, he could have killed frail Willy!

The man spoke to the two boys sharply for a minute and then went on his way. Felicidad grabbed Willy by the hand to lead him home, scolding him all the while, and the blond boy, with his head up in the air, went directly to the house right next door to theirs.

Felicidad noticed that this house and the one on the other side of it were different from the rest of the block. They were freshly painted in a pretty shade of gray, and each had a beautiful red door with a shiny brass knocker on it. Their iron gates were clean, and their steps were washed. The areaways were spotless. They must have a better landlord than we have, Felicidad thought, or maybe they're very rich.

The blond boy stared at them balefully while he waited for someone to let him in. Then he suddenly let out a whoop of joy as a bright-blue sports car drew up in front of his house, and a young man, about eighteen or twenty years old, who looked very much like the boy, jumped out. It must be his brother, Felicidad thought.

After a few words with the boy, the young man turned to Felicidad and Willy and smiled at them apologetically. "I'm sorry," he said. "My kid brother here loves to fight—you know the way boys are. But don't mind what he says; he doesn't mean it."

The young man was so good-looking and his smile so warm and friendly that Felicidad couldn't help but smile back at him shyly. "I don't understand," she murmured in Spanish, but she added, *"gracias, gracias. . . .* Say you're sorry," she whispered to Willy, but he kept his head down and refused to say anything.

Felicidad thought this was the handsomest young man she'd ever seen in her life. He could have been a movie star, with his even white teeth, his blue eyes, and his cheeks pink from the cold. As she watched him take out a key and open the door for his brother and himself, she had a glimpse inside of soft rugs and pretty things. Even through the window you could see a bowl of yellow flowers and a beautiful shiny lamp behind the white organdy curtains.

The house where Felicidad and her family lived looked even worse now in comparison, and she felt an unfamiliar prick of irritation as she glanced down the long list of names inside the door and noticed that they were all Spanish names. Vague things she had heard at home came back to her. "The Puerto Ricans are treated badly in New York; nobody likes them." Thoughtfully she pressed the Esteves' bell and followed Willy inside.

"How could you get into a fight?" she asked him, as

they trudged up the stairs. "Your first day here, and with someone you don't even know! What are people going to think of you, coming into a strange city and fighting right away? What happened? Tell me."

Willy's face was sullen. "He called me names. I was just standing there. He called all Puerto Ricans bad names."

"What kind of names?"

"I'm not going to tell you. He used bad words."

"Did he call you them in Spanish or English?"

"Both."

Felicidad was silent and worried as they came into the apartment. What would her mother say?

Both Mrs. Marquez and Mrs. Esteves were shocked when they saw Willy. They scolded him excitedly, while Mrs. Marquez washed off his face and made sure he wasn't hurt. But they couldn't get anything out of him other than the statement that the boy next door had called him bad names.

"I know that boy. The whole family is stuck-up." Mrs. Esteves laughed. "They're good and mad, because they spent so much money fixing up those two houses and now Puerto Ricans live next door. They don't like it. The lady, Mrs. Duncan, stopped me on the street one day and asked me if I'd clean her house for her. I wanted to spit in her face, but I was very polite. I said no thank you, that I had enough work cleaning my own house. Her sister lives next door in the other house.

She's Mrs. Benton, a nice lady . . . *señora buena.* She has a little baby, and always asks me if I know a baby sitter. Maybe you'll baby-sit for her, Felicidad. She'll pay you good."

"You keep away from that boy. You hear me?" Mrs. Marquez said to Willy. "I don't care what he says to you, you just walk away and don't listen. Understand?"

Reluctantly Willy promised.

"He'll be all right when he goes to school," Mrs. Esteves said. "The men get too hotheaded up here. They're always afraid someone's going to make a fool of them, and quick, they're ready to fight. At home nobody fights, but up here they go a little crazy—they're different. I don't let anyone put anything over on me, but I get along fine wherever I go. In New York it's like any other place—some good people, some bad people. You just have to learn to stay away from the bad ones."

"Is that boy's brother—the older one—is he stuck-up too?" Felicidad asked timidly.

Mrs. Esteves threw back her head and laughed heartily. "Oh, so you saw *him* too! Well, don't get any ideas in your head about him. He wouldn't look at a Puerto Rican girl for dirt. If he did, his mother would kill him."

"He seemed very nice," Felicidad said defensively. "Besides, I'm not interested in boys very much," she lied. "Come on. Aren't we going shopping?"

Chapter 7

❦

Warily, Felicidad stretched her legs in the double bed. If she stuck to the warm spots that Margarita had just vacated, she'd be all right. Through the thin walls she could hear the whir of Mr. Garcia's electric razor next door. It must be five minutes to eight, because at eight o'clock Mr. Garcia would finish shaving, and he would open the door of his apartment and, in his high Spanish voice, shout into the hall, "Is the bathroom empty, please?"

This was the routine he went through every morning. No one ever answered him. Mrs. Esteves said she had once made the mistake of being in the bathroom at that time, and the mild-mannered Mr. Garcia had gone into such a rage, accusing her of causing him to lose his job, that she'd rather die than be in his way again. All his morning preparations were accompanied by his singing *Madre Mia* at the top of his voice, always the same words, with no variation. He would stop only to curse the cold weather and to speak to his electric razor as if it were a beloved friend. "There, there, *querida mia*. Now take it easy."

Mrs. Marquez said it would be better if he bought shoes for his children instead of an expensive electric razor for himself, but Felicidad could understand how Mr. Garcia felt. She felt exactly the same way about the fleecy red robe she had bought. Her mother had said it was too expensive and that a coat was more important, but Felicidad had wanted that robe more than anything else in the world. Finally she had bought it and had settled on a short, warm jacket instead of a real coat. Her mother said that half of her would freeze all winter, but she didn't care. Now she slept with the robe carefully spread over her feet, and whenever she was in the house, she usually put it on—even over her clothes—to keep her warm. The very color of it made her feel good.

This was Carlos and Margarita's early week, and she could hear them in the kitchen—talking, talking. Where did they find so much to talk about?

Felicidad recognized other sounds as they floated in on her sleepy consciousness. The loud, grinding noise of the garbage trucks. (Had Willy remembered to carry down their overflowing bags of garbage?) The radio blasting away in the Martines' apartment below her, and Willy and the young Negro boy, Danny Smith, already playing a noisy game in the hall. These noises were very different from the song of the little *coqui!* (Would there be a letter from Fernando today?)

Danny Smith. . . . That meant her mother would look stern and tight-lipped at breakfast. It gave her a funny feeling the way her mother hated Danny Smith.

Danny was the only friend Willy had found in the two weeks since they had landed in New York. He was a round-faced, bright-eyed boy, about six months older than Willy, and Willy had formed a great attachment for him. The two boys were together before Danny went off to school and again after he returned home in the afternoon. Danny's family was the only non-Spanish family in the tenement, but Danny knew a little Spanish and was rapidly teaching Willy English.

Mrs. Marquez, however, had been frowning on the friendship ever since it started. She said Danny was too old for Willy, that he hung out on the street too much, and that he didn't speak nicely. She kept finding one thing wrong with him after another. However, Felicidad knew that one reason that her mother didn't like him was because his father was their janitor, whom she called "a lazy good-for-nothing." But mainly, she disliked him because he was a southern colored boy.

It was something Felicidad could not understand. Her mother herself did not reason it out, nor could she possibly explain it or try to put it into words. It wasn't the color of Danny's skin that bothered her. Although

Mrs. Marquez and Felicidad had very fair skin, Carlos and Willy were both quite dark, and at home, colors varied so much that it mattered very little what color anyone was. But Mrs. Marquez did take great pride in her Spanish blood, and she knew that the Negroes in the States were way down on the social scale—it was pretty apparent to her even right here in their house— and she resented Willy's choosing Danny for his first and only friend. If she had thought about it at all, she would have felt sorry about the way Negroes were treated, but instinctively she did not want herself or any other member of her family—or the Puerto Ricans in general, for that matter—to be lumped together with the Negroes by the white population of New York.

Only the night before, the whole situation had come out in the open. Willy had announced he was eating supper downstairs with the Smiths. They were having southern fried chicken and corn pone, two things Willy had never eaten before, and Mrs. Smith had asked him to stay. But when he came upstairs to tell his mother, Mrs. Marquez uttered a clear, determined no, and then closed her mouth firmly.

Willy's face fell, and he started begging, but his mother's face warned him to stop. "You are picking up bad ways from him already," she said. "Spanish children do not beg their parents. They obey quietly and nicely."

"I'm not Spanish, I'm American," Willy retorted quickly.

"Yes, yes, of course you are American," his mother said. "But don't forget that you come from an old and fine Spanish family. You are Latin-American. Your great-grandfather was in the employ of a nobleman. He was the trusted friend of Count Vázquez Vélez. He was the overseer for his farm of one-hundred-and-seventy acres, and when I visited Spain I was a guest in the home of the Count and Countess. Just don't forget who you are. You cannot run around with any child you pick up on the streets. I do not know Mr. and Mrs. Smith, so how can you go there to eat?"

"Oh Mother, you know Mr. Smith. He cleans the hall, and he collects the garbage."

"He's supposed to, but he doesn't," she said tartly. "I don't want to talk about it any more."

Mrs. Esteves and Felicidad had been silent throughout the conversation, although all of them were in the kitchen together. As soon as Willy went back to his room, looking as if he was going to cry, Mrs. Esteves said gently, "What's wrong with his having supper there? Mrs. Smith is a very nice woman. Once in a while her husband does forget to pick up the garbage. But so what? He has to work all day, and sometimes he even takes on a night shift to get along. They don't pay him anything to take care of this dump. Maybe he has free rent, but they couldn't get anyone to pay rent for that hole down in the basement anyway. And she keeps it spotless. Let the boy go. It's nice he has a friend. He's learning English, and when he goes to school it'll be easier for him."

"I don't think he's a good playmate for my Willy," Mrs. Marquez said stubbornly. "I've always been fussy about whom my children go with, and I don't intend to change now."

"She doesn't like him because he's colored," Felicidad said abruptly. She could feel herself getting hot inside with indignation. "Mother, this is New York City, and you'd better not be so stuck-up. We're all in the same boat!"

Her mother's face was shocked. "You never talked to me like that before! If this is what you and Willy are learning in New York, we'd better go right home."

"It is different here from the way it is back home," Mrs. Esteves said placatingly. "I suppose we have to learn new ways too. But maybe Felicidad is partly right. Maybe you don't like him because he is colored. And that isn't right. The people next door—they hate us because we're Puerto Ricans. You hate the Smiths because they're colored. Where does it all end? I suppose the Smiths hate all the white people, whether they're Puerto Ricans, Spanish, Americans, or anything. Why should we all hate each other? It is no good."

"I don't like living in a house with colored people,"

Mrs. Marquez said. "If you had told me that, I wouldn't have come here to live."

"Oh dear! That is exactly what the New Yorkers say when the Puerto Ricans move into their houses." Mrs. Esteves shook her head sadly.

"I think you should let Willy go," Felicidad said boldly. "And he should start going to school, too. I'm going to take him tomorrow." She looked at her mother defiantly. It was true, she had never spoken to her mother like this before, but she felt she had to. It gave her a new, exciting feeling of being grown-up. "And I'm going out to look for a job, too."

Her mother had been putting off sending Willy to school. She was afraid he would get lost or that something would happen to him. Also, she wouldn't listen to Felicidad whenever she said she had to find a job. "You don't know any English yet," her mother argued, "and you'll get lost going out alone."

The truth was, her mother was really afraid of the city, with all the thousands of cars and the noise and all the strange people speaking a language she couldn't understand. But Felicidad was eager to get started. She hadn't come to New York to stay cooped up in a kitchen with her mother, Mrs. Esteves, and Willy. Even Mrs. Esteves, who had been living here now for almost a year, spoke only Spanish and didn't venture very far from the block, far west on Twentieth Street, where they lived.

Willy had not gone down to the Smiths for supper, but waking up now, Felicidad decided to carry through her statements of the night before. She was going to take Willy to school, and she was going to go out by herself and find a job. Carlos and Margarita had inquired up at the hotel where they worked, but there was nothing there. As a matter of fact, they were laying off help, and both Carlos and Margarita were afraid they would lose their jobs.

Last night Felicidad had looked through the paper Carlos had brought home with him—the English one, not the Spanish one—and she had seen many jobs open for waitresses. She knew how to wait on tables, because once in a while she had helped out in the inn back home in Barranquitas, and she had felt a wave of confidence when she saw how many restaurants were looking for help. It took her a long time to read the English —it was slow going—but she had marked off a list of places where she could look. Then she had tried to find their location on the map of New York that Mrs. Esteves had pinned up on the kitchen wall. The east and west streets weren't so hard to find, but the numbers on the avenues were impossible, for she didn't know what street they came out on.

Now she jumped out of bed, and the first thing she did was to stick her head out of the door and call down the stairs to Willy. Her mother abhorred people's calling through the halls, and Felicidad realized this was something she would never have done at home. But then she hadn't lived in this kind of a house in Puerto Rico, filled with so many families. Besides, everybody else did it, so it became easier than going up and down two long flights of stairs.

"Willy, come right upstairs and get ready for school. I'm going to take you this morning."

"O.K., O.K." This was Willy's brand-new word, and his favorite one in English. He said "O.K." to everything, whether he meant it or not. He kept telling Felicidad to speak to him in English, but she still felt shy about it, and she didn't know enough words. Besides, she thought in Spanish, and it came much more easily. Actually, so far there had been no need for her to worry about her English. The Esteves saw no one but Puerto Ricans. The little grocery store where they shopped was owned by a Puerto Rican, and everyone in the house— except the Smiths—never spoke anything but Spanish. English was just a strange language you heard on the streets, and only once in a while was Felicidad able to catch a word that she understood.

"I'm taking Willy to school this morning," she announced in the kitchen to her mother and to Mrs. Esteves. "And then I'm going to look for a job."

Mrs. Marquez had a resigned look on her face. "God wills it," she said. "But how is Willy going to come home? He'll get killed crossing the streets."

"Danny'll bring him home. Don't worry."

"A fine thing for Willy to have to be taken care of by someone like Danny!"

Felicidad wanted to scold her mother, but she held her tongue. Her mother's eyes looked so sad and bewildered that Felicidad knelt down beside her and hugged her instead. Her mother used to be gay and full of fun, like Mrs. Esteves, and Felicidad couldn't help worrying about her. Perhaps she and Carlos had pushed too much upon her. She hadn't even recovered from the shock of her husband's death when they moved her up north, but then they had thought hopefully that the change would do her good.

But Felicidad couldn't stay depressed long, especially today. It was too exciting to think of going out by herself to find a wonderful job! Then she'd have money, and she could cheer her mother up. The salaries she'd read in the paper sounded like a lot of money just for waiting on tables. Soon they'd go up to Radio City, and then she would take her mother down to the wonderful store on Fourteenth Street, and maybe she'd buy a television set!

Felicidad dressed herself in the new clothes they had bought on her first day in New York—a slim, mustard-colored wool skirt and a bright-red jersey. Her mother had fussed about the colors, saying they were far too bright, and also about the skirt's being much too tight, but Felicidad had noticed other girls in the store wearing things just like that, and more than anything in the world she wanted to look like the girls in the States. She had never seen so many clothes to choose from in her life. In the store they had visited there were racks and racks of dresses, and the store itself seemed to be blocks long. Back home in Barranquitas they had sometimes ordered from a mail-order catalogue, but most of the time Felicidad had made her own clothes or bought something ready-made at the little store on the plaza.

Her ankles wobbled in her high heels, and Mrs. Esteves laughed at the way she walked. "You'd better be careful. I don't know how you'll get on a bus, with that tight skirt and those high heels!"

"She looks like a girl of twenty-one or twenty-two," Mrs. Marquez remarked critically, "not like a proper, nice young girl."

"That's good. That'll make it easier for me to get a job," Felicidad answered good-naturedly. "I want to look older."

"Don't talk to anybody—no strangers at all," Mrs. Marquez warned her again before she and Willy left. "Do you think you can find your way back here all right?" she asked anxiously.

"Yes, don't worry. I'll be fine." Felicidad kissed her mother and Mrs. Esteves good-by.

Mrs. Esteves handed her a piece of paper with their

address carefully printed on it. "Here. Take this. And if you get lost, just ask a policeman—a man in a blue uniform. You know what a policeman looks like?"

"Yes, yes." Felicidad was anxious to be off, and she followed Willy down the steps. She would have liked to run down quickly the way he did, but she did have to walk carefully in the high heels and the tight skirt. Before she stepped out into the cold, she buttoned up her jacket and tied a purple silk scarf around her head.

If she lived in New York a million years she would never get used to the cold. Each time she stepped out of the house it hit her anew. This morning it seemed worse than ever, but perhaps she had not been out this early before. The cold was bitter, and the wind wrapped itself cruelly around her legs. Perhaps her mother had been right about Felicidad's buying a long coat. The whole lower half of her *was* freezing! But there was nothing she could do about it now.

Determinedly she grasped Willy's hand. "Stay right with me," she told him. Her heart was fluttering as they crossed the wide avenue. The way the cars darted around corners without any warning, you could get hit in a second! She and Willy ran until they reached the other side.

Willy already knew where the school was, and led Felicidad to it. Her heart fell when she saw it. It was not what she had imagined. It looked like a prison, not a bit like a school. The big, drab, colorless building,

with iron grates across its dirty windows, had cement
all around it. There was no grass to play on—no place
to play at all. It was a forbidding and frightening place
to have to enter. She held on tighter than ever to
Willy's hand, her heart hammering. She wondered if
he was as scared as she was. At least she didn't have to
stay—but to leave Willy in this place! A look at his
white face filled her with pity, and for a wild moment
she thought maybe it would be better not to have him
go to school at all. But maybe it would be better inside;
maybe it would be prettier and friendlier. . . .

If anything, the inside was worse than the outside.
There were soiled, battleship-gray corridors and closed
doors. Through a little pane of glass in the doors you
could see the classrooms, with everyone sitting stiffly in
his seat, two children to a seat, and so crowded on top
of each other that you wondered how they could even
write. And the classrooms were as drab and colorless as
the rest of the building, with the monotonous voices of
tired-looking women droning away in front of the children.

Felicidad thought of the pink stucco building where
she and Willy had gone to school back home. Hibiscus
flowers grew outside the building—you could reach out
the windows and touch them or look out at the trees
and the blue sky. And young, jolly Mrs. Martinez, who
waddled a little when she walked, had filled her classroom with all kinds of growing things—plants and tiny

toads and lizards. Colored pictures of all kinds were stuck around the walls. Mrs. Martinez loved color. She came to school wearing the brightest dresses imaginable, and you felt happy just coming into her classroom.

Felicidad didn't know where to go in this huge building, and she and Willy stood in the corridor awkwardly, until finally Felicidad got up the courage to knock on one of the closed doors. A teacher's voice called out, telling them to come in.

Felicidad went in, holding Willy's hand, and shyly announced in Spanish that he wanted to come to school. The whole class burst out laughing. Felicidad's face turned a fiery red, and she wished the floor would open up and close over her. There was a sick smile on her lips, and she felt even worse when the teacher rapped sharply on her desk with a ruler and scolded the class for laughing.

She then ordered a very dark, small Puerto Rican boy in the front row to take them somewhere. He got up willingly, and once they were outside the room, Felicidad asked him in Spanish where they were going. He explained he had to take them to the principal's office and that the principal would send Willy to the right classroom. He also offered the information that this teacher was the worst one in the school and that the principal was a man and wasn't half bad. At least *he* could speak a little Spanish, but the classes were all in

English, and they were a pain in the neck. Half the time, he said, he didn't know what was going on, but he didn't care, because he didn't like school anyway.

The boy took them to the door of the principal's office and left them standing there while he went back to his classroom. Felicidad pulled down her skirt, adjusted the scarf on her head, and holding Willy's hand firmly in her own, knocked on the door timidly. A man's voice told them to come in.

Mr. Adams really was nice. He had a friendly smile, and he asked them to sit down. He spoke Spanish quite well for a Continental, Felicidad thought, and he asked Willy a few questions about how old he was and what class he had been in back home and what he had been studying.

Then he said he'd put him in the sixth grade. While it might be a little young for him, he said, it would be better and easier for him until he learned more English.

Willy said he didn't care what class he was put into, but Felicidad felt worried when Mr. Adams explained that Willy would be in school only in the mornings, because they had double sessions.

"But what will he do all afternoon?" Felicidad asked. "We thought he'd be in school all day until three o'clock, the way he is at home."

Mr. Adams shook his head sadly. "That's what we'd like to do, but we don't have enough schools for all the children. So some come in the afternoon and some in the morning."

Felicidad thought it very odd that a country as rich as the United States didn't have enough schools. In her little island there were schools everywhere, and the rooms weren't crowded and dreary the way they were here. But she was much too polite and shy to say anything.

She felt sad as she left Willy at the door of the classroom. "I hope you find Danny to come home with. Remember, he promised to wait for you right outside. Take care. And Willy, no fighting."

He looked much too scared to do anything, and with a heavy heart, she finally left him.

Chapter 8

Outside, the cold and the wind had not abated. Felicidad walked as quickly as she could in her high heels and tight skirt. She stayed close to the buildings, hoping they would protect her from the wind, and waited in the doorway of a drugstore for a bus that would take her uptown to the first place on her list for a job.

She showed the bus driver the address and, in her faltering English, asked him please to let her know where to get off. He answered her in rapid English, which she didn't understand, and the bus stopped so abruptly that she almost fell into a strange man's lap. She didn't know what to do, until fortunately, a Puerto Rican man told her in Spanish that she was on the wrong bus. He told her to get off and walk over two blocks. Without even trying to get her fare back, she got off the bus as soon as it stopped, and trudged in the cold once more.

At last she found herself on the right bus, and she got off at Madison Avenue and Forty-sixth Street, a neighborhood that was very different from the part of New York she had seen so far. Here there were mostly big buildings and beautiful shops and very grand-looking fur coats on the women who walked by.

Felicidad pulled her scarf tighter under her chin. She stopped in a doorway to powder her nose, although her mother had often told her this was something a lady never did in public. But she didn't care. She wanted to be sure she looked all right before she went to see about the job.

At the self-service elevator she stopped, because she was afraid to go in alone. She felt shy about asking a man for help, so she waited until a young girl came along. Then she showed her the clipping she'd torn from the newspaper. It clearly said, *Seventeenth floor*. Luckily the girl understood what she wanted, and she got into the elevator with her and pushed the button. Up they went. Felicidad had never been in an elevator before, and her heart was in her mouth until it stopped. She was glad to get out and wondered how she would ever get down again, but she'd worry about that later. First, the job.

She walked into a waiting room that was filled with girls and women. Were they all after the same job? A very pretty blond woman sat at a desk in the middle of the room and coolly handed Felicidad a number. She motioned to her to sit down and wait.

Felicidad felt as if all eyes were on her. As she sat

on a deep, low chair, her skirt slithered up over her knees, and she frantically tried to pull it down. Self-consciously, she undid the scarf around her head. The other girls were either bareheaded or had on hats. Timidly, she kept her eyes down, but every once in a while she glanced swiftly around the room to see if there were any other Puerto Rican girls she could possibly talk to. But none of the girls looked Spanish, and English was all that was being spoken. She wished she knew how to smoke. She envied the girls who were puffing on one cigarette after another.

There was no restaurant in sight way up here, and it seemed odd to be looking for a job as a waitress in a place like this. Carefully, she read the ad from the newspaper over again, and she realized this must be an office for a chain of restaurants. Good. That meant more jobs.

She sat for an hour and a half before her number was called, and when her turn finally came, she was so sleepy she came to with a start. The girls who were still waiting laughed when she suddenly jumped up, and Felicidad blushed a fiery red.

Nervously she followed the girl who had come for her, down a long corridor and then into a large, cheerful room. Here an older woman sat at a desk and greeted her with a fixed smile. "Good morning. Sit down." In her hand she had a card that Felicidad had filled out in the waiting room. "I see you worked at an inn in Puerto Rico. You Puerto Rican?" the woman asked.

Felicidad nodded her head. "Yes," she said in English.

"I'm so sorry, but the jobs are all taken."

Felicidad looked up and caught the woman's blue eyes looking at her. She knew instantly that the woman was lying. She didn't know how she knew, but she did.

"I speak some English, and I know how to wait good," Felicidad said.

"I'm sorry. The jobs are all filled up." She dismissed Felicidad with a curt nod. Felicidad walked back down the corridor and saw all the other girls still waiting to be interviewed. She had sat there for an hour and a half, and the whole thing had taken less than a minute!

Flushing with shame, anger, and humiliation, Felicidad went through the waiting room hurriedly and back to the elevators. There was no one else waiting for an elevator, but she couldn't bear to wait until another girl came out, and she was terrified to get into one of those things alone. She might press the wrong button. Heaven alone knew what might happen! Desperately, she looked for the stairs and saw a door with a little red light over it. Felicidad opened it and gratefully welcomed the flight of stairs.

Seventeen . . . sixteen . . . fifteen. . . . It was a nightmare walking down all those floors. She thought she'd never come to the end of them, never! She was only thankful that she didn't have to face another human being on the way. When at last she reached the bottom she sat down on the steps, ready to weep. The image of that woman's cold blue eyes kept glaring at her, and she heard her sweet, polite voice. "I'm sorry. The jobs are all taken...."

Felicidad took her scarf out of her bag, combed out her hair, and put it up again, wrapped in the scarf. She powdered her face and retouched her mouth with lipstick. There were five more places to go—she couldn't give up yet. Surely there'd be a job for her somewhere.

But one after another, the excuses came. She didn't have enough experience, or she was too young, or the jobs were already taken. But in her heart, Felicidad knew in each place that they didn't want her because she was a *puertorriqueña*. Otherwise, why were all the other girls waiting? They were just as young as she. They couldn't have that much experience. If the jobs were really filled they'd send them all home. And the way the people looked at her—apologetic, pretending to be truly sorry! But all the while, their eyes were saying, "You poor little fool! Don't you know we don't hire Puerto Ricans around here? We want our own, and you're not one of us."

You're not one of us! But I'm an American too, Felicidad thought fiercely. I don't want to be Puerto Rican, I want to be *American*. And I'm going to speak and look and think exactly like you—you wait and see!

It was the end of the day, and she got on an over-crowded bus to go back home. She was downhearted and discouraged, but something in her was very, very angry, too. She'd show them. She wouldn't *let* them treat her this way! She elbowed and pushed her way through the crowded bus. All these girls and men and women coming home from jobs! She didn't care if she stepped on that fat woman's foot—served her right for having it there. And with a total, illogical fierceness she hated the whole busload of people. She hated them all.

She got off the bus at Twenty-third Street and faced the long, windy blocks across town toward home. As she turned down Ninth Avenue, a little sign in the dirty window of a dingy lunchroom caught her eye. It was in Spanish. *"Yo necesito una muchacha que trabaje."* Waitress needed. She knew without looking up at the name over the door that it was a Puerto Rican restaurant. Well, they'd have a job for her here.

With a sigh of resignation, she went in and spoke to the owner. He was no cleaner than his store—a small, dark man, with a carefully tended mustache and most of him covered by a soiled white apron. She took Margarita's advice and lied about her age, saying she was over eighteen. He hired her right away and told her to come to work the following day at twelve noon. The salary he mentioned was less than half that offered by the clean, beautiful places uptown, and the hours were longer. The place smelled of stale food, but it was familiar Puerto Rican food, and the customers spoke only Spanish, so that part of it was a relief.

"O.K.," Felicidad said. "I'll be here," she added in Spanish.

She was tired, and she walked home slowly. How do you become a New Yorker? she wondered. How do you learn English? How do you learn new ways if you must all huddle together in your own little corners?

Perhaps Fernando was right. Perhaps they would be better off staying home on their own little island, sticking to their own ways, even if they were old-fashioned. As always, when she thought of Fernando, her heart filled with a great longing to see him and to be at home. He and home were part of each other, and she wondered if the sun was shining brightly today and if Fernando was even now out in the fields with his machete and what tune he would be whistling. Neither one of them was much at letter writing, so the letters were few and far between.

But Fernando is stubborn, she thought. He'll never know what the rest of the world looks like. We're here, and I *did* get a job, and Carlos *is* making money, and Willy *is* going to an American school. . . .

Willy! Remembering Willy, she hurried her steps, worrying about whether he had got home all right. She'd completely forgotten about him and his first day of school.

She was exhausted, but she went up the stairs quickly

and walked into the kitchen. This was the only living room the apartment had, and everyone stayed there, except when it was time to sleep. Immediately, from her mother's face, she knew something unpleasant had happened. Willy was sitting and staring out the window, while her mother walked about the kitchen, nervously picking up a speck of dirt here and there and putting it down again. Mrs. Esteves was preparing rice and beans for supper, although Margarita, Carlos, and Mr. Esteves never got home until late, because they had to work through dinnertime at the hotel.

"Where were you all day? I was worried sick about you," her mother said accusingly.

"I told you I was going out to look for a job," Felicidad said.

"Did you get one?" her mother asked her sharply.

"Yes." Felicidad drew herself up proudly. The look of disbelief on her mother's face hurt her as much as anything that had happened all day. So her mother thought she couldn't get a job! "And a good one too," she added, lying calmly. No one would ever know what she had suffered this day, and she was suddenly determined also that her mother would never know she was working at a cheap, greasy Puerto Rican restaurant. She'd make up more details later, when she had a chance to think, and if her mother asked her, she'd tell her she was working for a beautiful New York restaurant uptown.

"That's very good," Mrs. Esteves said cheerfully. "It's O.K."

"What's the matter with you, Willy? How was school?" His face was so woebegone Felicidad almost didn't want to hear his answer. She couldn't bear any more unpleasantness this day.

And Willy's story was not a happy one. His mother answered for him. "He lost his new coat," she said, and her eyes were tragic. "His brand-new coat. He hung it up in the coatroom, and it's gone. What kind of a city is this? They steal a little boy's brand-new coat! The teacher said she couldn't do anything. . . . You children haven't been to Mass—that's the trouble. That's why everything is no good."

"But who would steal your coat, Willy?" Felicidad asked in consternation. "What a terrible thing to do!"

"What do they care!" Mrs. Esteves said bitterly. "A Puerto Rican kid doesn't need a coat! They'll steal anything from him they can get. And then they say he makes the trouble. Willy, you'll have to learn how to take care of yourself up here. Don't be afraid to fight if you have to."

Mrs. Marquez was shocked by this advice. "No, you mustn't fight, Willy. Someone will stab you with a knife. But don't put your coat down anyplace. Just hold on to it. Keep it with you—on your seat by your desk."

"Ma, I haven't got any coat now. And if I get one, I

gotta put it in the coatroom. The teacher says so." He shrugged his shoulders. "What can I do?"

"Felicidad will go to school with you tomorrow and see if she can find the coat," Mrs. Marquez ordered.

Felicidad was too tired to argue. But her mother didn't understand any part of it. She didn't know what it really meant to be living up here. Felicidad wondered idly if she'd ever find out. Her mother thought it was all Willy's fault, and if she knew the kind of job Felicidad had taken, she'd say that was Felicidad's own fault too, that she was forgetting to keep her head high. Wearily, she set the table for their supper. But it wasn't their fault, not hers or Willy's.

It was the fault of all the other people in the city. They were making the mistake. They were doing the hating. And she hated them in return.

With an uncontrollable feeling of contempt, she took the bag of garbage Mrs. Esteves had asked her to put outside, and she threw it out the window. She watched it land gently all over the sidewalk, and for an instant it made her heart feel quiet and strong. But when she realized what a foolish, mean thing she'd done, she went into the bedroom, closed the door behind her, and shed the tears she had been holding back all day.

Chapter 9

Felicidad did not go to school with Willy the next morning. In order to avoid a fuss with her mother, she left with him and walked as far as the school building. But when she saw that forbidding place and the enormous mob of children pouring into it, she felt it would be useless to go inside. They'd never find his coat anyway. No one was going to admit he stole it, and certainly no one was going to bring it back. So she said good-by to poor Willy, who was shivering in a sweater belonging to Carlos, which was at least two sizes too big for him.

Walking back home, she was trying to think of what to say to her mother about Willy's coat, when the full impact of what she was doing suddenly occurred to her. It wasn't only that she was telling her mother a lie. She had told lies before—small, unimportant ones, to be sure—and had confessed them to Father Sebastian and had done penance for them. But now she was making decisions without consulting any parent.

It gave her an odd feeling both of being grown-up and of doing something wicked and frightening. She had made the decision about taking the job without asking her mother, and she knew very well her mother would never approve of the place where she would be working. And now she had decided on her own to disobey her mother about going in to speak to the teacher about Willy's coat! What had happened in the short time they had been in New York?

Father Sebastian had spoken to them often about honoring and respecting their parents and about not falling in with the ways of some young people—especially those in the States—who ignored their elders and thought that they themselves knew everything. But it *was* different up here. Her mother just stayed in the house or went out to the store with Mrs. Esteves. She didn't know anything about what went on. It wasn't the same as at home, where her mother knew everyone and knew how things should be done.

Felicidad felt an unfamiliar weight of responsibility lying heavily upon her and wondered if she was doing the right thing. At the same time she had a sense of thrilling excitement. She wanted to be a real American New Yorker more than anything else in the world, and she felt that having your parents make all the decisions was a Latin way, not an American one.

It was a relief that Father Sebastian wasn't here to admonish her, but she did have a great desire to go to church. There had been rather a battle in the household about that matter ever since they had arrived. The Esteves family went to a place down the block from them that wasn't really a church at all. The congregation met in an empty store. It was called a "store-front church," and had the name of *Iglesia Cristiana de Jerusalém*. Its services were very different from the Catholic ritual that Felicidad was used to. They had all gone once with the Esteves, but Mrs. Marquez refused to go again, and she scolded Carlos continually for going with Margarita. Mrs. Marquez had found a Roman Catholic church about four or five blocks from their house, and she went to Mass every morning, even on the coldest days. However, Felicidad had gone with her only once or twice.

Now she approached the church and went inside. It was empty and quiet, and Felicidad felt a terrible wave of homesickness overtake her. She dipped her finger into the holy water, made the sign of the Cross, and genuflected. Staying in the back of the church, she slipped into a pew and knelt down. Everything was so different here. There was no sunlight coming through the windows of this church, the way it did at home. But little by little, the familiar things about it took hold. The Blessed Mother was close, and Jesus was here, the same as He was at home. Felicidad prayed fervently that she would have guidance in this strange, big city and that she would be given strength to hold her temper and not to hate or fall into bad ways. Before she left, she resolved to come back later to see the priest for confession and went out, feeling considerably better.

When she returned to her block, the bright little sports car was parked in front of the house next door. The handsome blond boy got out and smiled. "Hello," he said. "No more fights, I hope."

She shook her head shyly. "No. My brother is in school now." She spoke hesitantly in English, very conscious of her accent.

"That's good. What about you? Aren't you going to school?"

"No—I work," she said.

"Lucky for you! I'd like to have a job, but I have to go to school. I'm going to college next year."

"That's good. Good." She nodded her head vigorously. "At home I would go to the university too. But not here. Here I work."

"Well, so long," he said abruptly. "Be seeing you." He gave her a bright, warm smile, but she followed his eyes to the front window of his house and saw the curtain move and a woman's figure quickly turn away. That must be his mother, and she had been beckoning him to come in. The boy flushed, and Felicidad realized that he did not want his mother to see him talking to her.

She ran into the house and all the way up the two

flights of stairs without stopping, until she flung herself down on a kitchen chair to get her breath. Her anger was rising up again, and she fought desperately to calm herself and to regain the quiet confidence she had had such a short while ago in church.

"What's the matter? Somebody chasing you?" Mrs. Esteves asked with a smile.

Felicidad shook her head. "No, but I ran up the stairs too fast," she said.

"What time do you start your job?" her mother asked her.

"Twelve o'clock."

"Then maybe you can run over to Mrs. Benton's this morning," Mrs. Esteves said. "She stopped me when I brought the garbage down and asked me if you'd like to baby-sit for her tonight. When do you get finished working?"

"Eight o'clock." Felicidad was silent for a moment. "Mrs. Benton—who's she?" she finally asked, although she knew perfectly well who she was.

"She's the sister of the woman next door. She lives in the next house over. She's O.K. *Señora buena.* Stop and let her know whether you're going to do it or not."

Felicidad went to her room and sat staring out of the window. She felt sulky and sullen. She didn't feel like baby-sitting for any stuck-up woman, and yet she wanted money badly. There were so many things she saw in the stores in New York that she wanted to buy.

After a while she went in to speak to her mother. "What do you think I should do?" she asked. "Should I baby-sit for her?"

Her mother shrugged her shoulders. "It's up to you. Why not? She'll pay you well."

Her mother had become thinner and paler since they had moved here. It was so cold that she hardly ever went out on the street, except to go to church, and sitting cooped up in the kitchen all day had given her a sallow, listless air that was different from the quick energy she had had at home. Felicidad felt unhappy and disappointed with her mother. Unhappy that she was so depressed, and disappointed, because she seemed to have no purpose or strength. Felicidad couldn't lean on her any more. Her mother was bewildered and helpless now.

And Carlos wasn't much good either. He was hardly ever around. When he and Margarita worked late, they slept all morning and got up just in time to rush out and back to work. And when they were on the earlier shift, they went out dancing or somewhere else right from work and didn't come home until late anyway. She didn't like to bother Mrs. Esteves, and she hardly ever saw Mr. Esteves. Besides, she would be too shy to ask him anything.

Felicidad cleaned up the bedrooms and fussed with her hair and her clothes until it was almost time to go to her new job. But she did allow herself a few minutes to stop in at Mrs. Benton's.

When she rang, Mrs. Benton herself answered the door and seemed very happy to see her. "Come in. I'm so glad to meet you. Mrs. Esteves has told me a great deal about you. You do understand English, don't you?"

"Very little," Felicidad said shyly, following her into a lovely, bright, sunny room. The room filled her with a nostalgia for home. While it was nothing like anything they had had, with its rich carpeting and upholstered sofas and chairs, it had color—one dark-red wall, bright pictures, and flowers everywhere. After all the drab, colorless streets and buildings and their own cheerless apartment, it was like walking into a garden back home.

Mrs. Benton looked a great deal like her handsome nephew, except that her eyes were brown instead of blue, and her skin had an olive cast to it that looked very pretty with her blond hair. But she held her back and head straight, the way he did, and she looked directly into your eyes when she spoke, and Felicidad liked her soft voice.

"Sit down." She sat on the sofa and motioned to Felicidad to sit beside her.

Felicidad was worried that she wouldn't be able to understand Mrs. Benton's English, but Mrs. Benton spoke slowly and clearly, and Felicidad could make out pretty well what she said. Her own answers were given falteringly, but Mrs. Benton said she was doing very well and that she must not be timid about her English. The only way she'd learn it was by using it, she said.

"Do you like New York?" Mrs. Benton asked her.

"*Si* . . . yes, it is very nice," Felicidad said politely. She certainly wasn't going to tell her that she thought the city was very dirty and too noisy, or that many people in it weren't nice. Like most Puerto Ricans, she was brought up to be very polite and to say yes to a great many things strangers asked, whether she really thought so or not. Mrs. Benton asked her about her job, and Felicidad politely said that that, too, was very nice.

They talked for a few minutes and arranged for Felicidad to come right from work at eight o'clock to take care of Mrs. Benton's little boy. Mrs. Benton brought him in—a curly-haired child, who fell in love with Felicidad's beads right away. This seemed to please Mrs. Benton enormously and to make her feel sure he would love Felicidad just as much.

Felicidad went back home to say good-by to her mother and to Mrs. Esteves. Then she nervously walked the four or five blocks to her first job in New York. It started snowing, a wet snow, and she pulled her collar up close to the scarf on her head. The first thing she would buy when she got paid, she made up her mind, would be a pair of those nice furry overshoes she saw so many of the girls wearing. Now her feet were getting soaked through the thin soles of her shoes, and her stockings were all splattered.

The restaurant looked even worse than she remembered it. When she had started out job hunting, she had had a vision of working in one of those beautiful restaurants that were all lit up. She had passed them on the bus and had had a peek inside of waitresses in crisp, pretty colored uniforms, covered with little ruffled aprons, and with bands on their hair. She would have met some New York girls and maybe become friends with them. But this place was nothing like that.

Along one wall there was a lunch counter, with booths opposite it and tables in between. It was crowded now, at lunch time, and everyone in the place was speaking Spanish. Since both the customers and the people who worked there all seemed to be Puerto Ricans, it made Felicidad feel at home, yet she longed to be able to meet some New York girls her own age, and have a chance to learn some English.

The man behind the lunch counter told her to go to the kitchen and report to the boss. In the kitchen Mr. Marin, the owner, set her to work at a huge pile of dirty dishes. "We're a little short today," he explained to Felicidad, when she said she thought she was supposed to be a waitress.

But the minute he went out of the kitchen the cook winked at Felicidad. "Don't believe a word he says," he told her. "He's a little short every day. You'll be lucky if you get to wait on tables once in a while."

The cook was a tall man for a Puerto Rican, with a beautiful smile and lovely hands. Obviously he had a good mixture of Indian blood in his veins. He was friendlier to Felicidad than anyone else. The other waitresses were too busy even to talk to her, until sometime in the middle of the afternoon, when the luncheon rush was over. Then the two girls, each of them a couple of years older than Felicidad, came into the kitchen, sat down with their legs stretched out, and lit up cigarettes. Felicidad was shocked to see them smoking, but she pretended to accept it as a matter of course.

One of the girls, whose name was Carmen, was very pretty, although Felicidad thought she had on far too much make-up. But she was intrigued as she watched her animated face, with all its swift, different expressions coming and going, like those of all Puerto Ricans. She spoke in Spanish very quickly, gesturing with her hands, and was continually putting one of them up to her hair, which had a beautiful red sheen to it and was exceptionally glossy and pretty. The other girl, Maria, was on the plump side, with a pretty face, but she was not as gay as her friend Carmen.

The two girls chatted a mile a minute, apparently about a date they'd been on the night before, when they had gone dancing at a place called *El Palacio*. Not knowing what to do with herself, Felicidad stood around uncomfortably, waiting for Mr. Marin, who was up front at the cash register, to come back and tell her what to do next.

Carmen turned to her and asked her if she had ever been to *El Palacio*. Felicidad shook her head. "I've never been out anyplace yet," she confessed. "I've only been here a few weeks."

"I was out dancing the second night I was in New York," Carmen said with a laugh. "We'll take you next time. O.K.?" she added in English. "We'll get you a date."

Felicidad's eyes shone. "I don't know if my mother will let me," she said.

Carmen and Maria both laughed. "Up here it's not the same as it is at home," Carmen said. "I don't *ask* my mother—I *tell* her what I'm doing. I'm eighteen, and I bring home money every week. She can't tell me what to do any more."

Felicidad had to digest this information and tuck it away in her mind to think about later. She was sure her mother would not approve of Carmen or Maria as suitable companions for her. And she would be horrified by the cigarettes! But Felicidad could not help liking these girls—especially Carmen. She was gay and full of fun and had a smile and a remark for all the people she waited on.

"The boys you go out with—are they Puerto Ricans or New Yorkers?" Felicidad asked.

Carmen looked at her in astonishment. "New York-ers? They don't bother with us. They go their way, we go ours. We *puertorriqueños* stay together."

"I came up here because I thought I'd meet *ameri-canos* from the States," Felicidad said wistfully. "I'd like to meet some boys and girls my age."

"Maybe if you went to school you would," Carmen said kindly. "But even there!" She shrugged her shoulders. "My kid sister—all her friends are the Puerto Rican kids who live in our house. We're better off when we stick to our own people. Don't you want to go out with a Puerto Rican boy?"

"Oh sure," Felicidad said hastily. "Of course I'd like to."

"Well, maybe we can find you a date with a New York boy," Carmen offered. "I'll ask my boy friend to bring along someone he works with."

Felicidad ate her supper at five with the other two girls, and then, in spite of what the cook had said, she did wait on tables. That was more fun than washing dishes, although it made Felicidad very nervous. Everyone was in such a hurry, and the cook took so much time about dishing out his servings, and the trays were so heavy and crowded with food, that Felicidad was terrified she'd drop one. But she got a few nice tips, and that made her feel very proud and pleased.

When she came outside again at eight o'clock, the streets were covered with snow. She had never walked in New York alone after dark before, and she felt very daring, as she tucked her scarf around her head and walked down Ninth Avenue.

The streets were quite deserted, except for groups of boys hanging around the corners in the snow, and Felicidad hurried past them without looking left or right. She had been warned dozens of times by Mr. Esteves to be careful when she was out alone, even in the daytime. "This is a wicked city," Mr. Esteves had said. "No one is safe. You be careful, Felicidad. Keep away from the boys, especially when there is a gang of them."

Every day they read in the Spanish papers about gang wars, and many of them were blamed on the Puerto Rican boys. Felicidad didn't believe that this was true, yet she was nervous—especially when she had to turn off the Avenue and into Twentieth Street, which was much darker. She ran down the street, slipping on the snow, past the dark doorways, where anyone or anything could be lurking. She heaved a sigh of relief when she reached the Benton house.

Mrs. Benton took her inside and made her take off her wet shoes and stockings and lent her a lovely pair of soft, fleecy, warm slippers to put on. She took her into little Freddie's room, where he was in his crib ready to go to sleep, and showed her where his things were, if he should need anything.

"There's milk in the refrigerator, and cookies," Mrs. Benton said. "Help yourself to what you want."

"I'll show you how to work the television," Mr. Benton added. He was a tall, quiet man, who reminded Felicidad of a doctor.

She said yes to everything that Mrs. Benton told her, but her kindness gave Felicidad an uneasy feeling. She couldn't help but feel suspicious of Mrs. Benton's gracious warmth. Why should she put herself out for a kid who was going to baby-sit for her, and especially for one of the hated Puerto Ricans from the tenement next door? At any minute Felicidad expected Mrs. Benton's true feelings to show, and her guard was up constantly.

"If anyone calls, please be sure to write down the name," Mrs. Benton said before leaving.

Felicidad nodded, although she hadn't really understood what Mrs. Benton said, and she was too shy, polite, and afraid to ask any questions.

When finally the door closed behind them, Felicidad breathed a sigh of relief. She made up her mind not to go near the refrigerator, because she was sure that no matter what she took, it would be the wrong thing. Besides, she didn't really believe they had left anything for her. But after sitting for a while, she did venture to turn on the television set. A dramatic show was being performed, and although she couldn't follow the English dialogue, she felt that trying to do it would be good for her. But it was boring to watch a show when you couldn't understand the words.

The phone rang, and she ran around frantically looking for it. Finally she answered it, saying, "No one home."

She started looking at the pictures in a magazine and jumped when there was a knock on the door. She stayed very quiet, hoping whoever was there would go away. But the knocking became insistent, and a male voice said, "It's Mrs. Benton's nephew from next door. May I come in, please?"

She recognized his voice, and she opened the door promptly. "I didn't want to let in any strangers," she said in Spanish.

"Oh." He was obviously surprised to see her. "Are you baby-sitting for my aunt? I didn't know. I came over to borrow a book I need. Can you understand my English?" he asked, as an afterthought.

Felicidad nodded her head. "A little. *Usted habla espanol?*" she asked him.

Jim laughed. "Very little. *Como se llama usted?*"

"*Me llamo Felicidad.* Felicidad Louisa Marquez," she said.

"*Muy linda.* Say, why don't you teach me Spanish, and I'll teach you English?" he said. "Don't you think that's a great idea?"

"Very good idea." She smiled at him. Since this was his aunt's house, she imagined it was all right for him to be here, but when he seemed to be making no effort to look for his book and settled himself down on the sofa instead, she wondered how her mother would like it.

It seemed odd for her to be all alone in a strange house with a strange boy. She had never been alone with a boy like this before in her life!

"Usted esta muy guapa," Jim said to her. "Do you know that?"

Felicidad blushed. *"Gracias,"* she said simply.

Jim got up and walked around the room restlessly. "I don't feel like doing homework," he said. "You girls are supposed to be wonderful dancers. Would you like to dance? I'll put on some music."

Felicidad shrugged her shoulders. She didn't know what to say. Somehow she felt it was wrong, but he was at home here, and she didn't feel that she could tell him what to do. He put on some records and again asked her to dance.

He was a beautiful dancer, and being a natural-born dancer herself, Felicidad couldn't help but relax in his arms. It was fun being with him—by far the most fun she'd had since she left home.

They couldn't have any real conversation because of the language problem, but they managed to talk together a little, and everything each of them said made them both laugh. Felicidad would start off trying to say something in English. Then when he looked perplexed, she'd try to make her meaning clear with gestures, until finally she'd go off into rapid Spanish, which sent Jim into gales of laughter. When he'd try to answer her in his faltering Spanish, she couldn't help but laugh too, at his New York accent and the mistakes he made.

"Do you like New York?" Jim asked her.

"Very nice," she said.

"You say 'very nice' to everything," he accused her. "I don't think you mean half of it. You can tell me the truth," he said coaxingly.

"It is very different from home," was all Felicidad would admit.

"I'll show you the real New York. I'd like to take you out and show you the theaters and the night clubs. We could have a lot of fun."

"I could not go out with you alone," Felicidad said. "My mother wouldn't permit me. We'd need a chaperon."

"You'd be safe with me. She wouldn't have to worry."

Felicidad didn't think so—not with the way he held her when they danced and the sure, sophisticated manner that he had. But she found it very exciting to be with him. He had such a grown-up air and evidently knew so much that he seemed older than the boys back home. And at the same time that she felt being with Jim was both wonderful and daring, she had an odd yearning for familiar Fernando.

Jim was still there with her when the Bentons came home, and they didn't seem to think anything of it. On the contrary, Mrs. Benton said, "How nice that Jim could keep you company."

Before Felicidad left, Mrs. Benton asked if anyone

had called, and unthinkingly, Felicidad said, "No." As far as she was concerned no one had called, since no message had been left.

The dank, stale smells in her own house seemed worse than ever after spending the evening at the Bentons'. Yet Felicidad felt it had been a strain to be there and to be with those people. She never knew what they were thinking, even Jim, and somehow she couldn't really trust them.

She sat down at the kitchen table and wrote a long letter to Fernando before she went to sleep. Barranquitas seemed very far away as she wrote, and she wished she could spend even one hour with Fernando, looking out over the misty, purple hills.

Chapter 10

It seemed just overnight to Felicidad and then, there
she was, part of Puerto Rican New York. She got up in
the morning, rushed off to the restaurant, worked hard
all day, came home, and spent her evenings with the
Puerto Rican friends that gathered in Mrs. Esteves'
kitchen, or went over to baby-sit for Mrs. Benton. It
was a life that was entirely different from what she had
had at home. Everyone and everything here were always in a hurry, and yet the routine had taken hold
so much that she felt she'd been in New York much
longer than just a few months. The time flew by
quickly, for many things seemed to be happening constantly.

The biggest change was being so much on her own.
It sometimes seemed as if she didn't have a family any
more, and it gave Felicidad an odd feeling. At home
they had always done everything together, but now all
of them seemed to be going their own separate ways.
There were times when Felicidad loved living this way,

and other times when she felt lost and worried—frightened mostly—and she missed seeing Willy and Carlos. She was usually asleep in the morning when Willy went off to school, and in the afternoons when he was out of school she was at work. But he wasn't often home either.

Her mother complained about Willy's never being at home, but Felicidad said she couldn't expect Willy to spend his afternoons gossiping in the kitchen with two women. He had to play with his friends and be with other children.

"But I don't know who his friends are—except Danny," Mrs. Marquez said helplessly. "I worry about him all the time."

"He's all right," Felicidad assured her. "Things are different here from what they are at home. All the kids play on the street alone, and they get along fine."

"They get along? They get into fights, and every day you read about stabbings and gang wars. I don't like it."

"Don't worry so much," Felicidad admonished her.

Mrs. Marquez was also worried about Carlos. "I don't understand what's happened to him. In Puerto Rico he never ran around; he stayed home like a good boy. Here, every night that he's not working, he comes in at three or four o'clock in the morning. One day he'll drop dead of exhaustion. He looks tired all the time, and pale and thin."

"He's in love," Felicidad said gaily. "He and Margarita haven't got time to sleep. They're too busy mooning at each other."

"Margarita's not the same girl she was at home. The way she smokes those cigarettes and goes out with Carlos alone! I think she even takes a drink when she's out with him. I'm surprised that Mrs. Esteves lets her do these things!"

"Mama, Mrs. Esteves couldn't stop her if she wanted to. Don't you understand that things are different up here? Girls aren't chaperoned, and they do smoke, and many of them drink. You're in New York, Mama—not in the village of Barranquitas."

Mrs. Marquez gave her daughter a sharp look. "You are not going to do those things, Felicidad. I'm warning you. I will not allow it."

Felicidad bent over and kissed her mother lightly on the cheek. "Don't worry about me, Mama. I'm all right."

But her mother's eyes followed her with a troubled look.

It was about a week after this conversation that Felicidad announced to her mother that Carmen was coming home with her from work the next evening. The girls had become very good friends on the job. Carmen was eighteen, two years older than Felicidad, and Felicidad thought she was the most sophisticated, glamorous girl she'd ever known—even more so than Margarita—because Carmen had lived in New York for four or five years up in *El Barrio* (Harlem), and every day she came to work with a new exciting story. She seemed to have dozens of boy friends. One week she'd be talking all about Joe, the next week it would be Luis, and then a few days later she'd come in, ecstatic about her latest one, Ramon. Ramon was still the current one, and Carmen was eager to have Felicidad meet him.

She also had all sorts of stories about the house where she lived. She called it a "rat-infested joint," and said it was filled with *ratas, cucarachas,* and *chinches.* She said there were always fights going on too. One morning she came in, pale-faced and excited, and told Felicidad and Maria about how a man living in their house had been stabbed.

"My mother's afraid to go out," Carmen confided, "and she doesn't want me to come home late at night any more. But I told her, 'What's the difference?' Around there you can get stabbed in the daytime, just as well as at night!"

The girls had planned an evening for Ramon to bring a friend along, and the two couples were to go dancing uptown at *El Palacio.* Afterward Felicidad wanted to stay overnight with Carmen, because she was curious to see *El Barrio,* and she also didn't want her mother to know how late she'd be getting home.

Nervously, but trying to be as casual as possible, Felicidad told her mother of her plans the night before the big event was to take place. She told her just a little bit at a time. First, she said that Carmen was coming home with her after work, because she wanted her mother to meet her.

"I'll be glad to have her," Mrs. Marquez said approvingly. "You talk about her so much! Besides, it is both my pleasure and my duty to meet your friends."

Felicidad wasn't at all sure that her mother would approve of Carmen. She would think her clothes were too flashy and that she used too much make-up, but there was nothing she could do about that. Later in the evening, when she thought her mother was in a good mood, Felicidad told her that she and Carmen were going out on a date with two boys.

"Carlos will go with you," Mrs. Marquez said promptly.

"Carlos can't come with us. He's working," Felicidad said, trying to keep calm. "Besides, it's perfectly all right. Carmen knows the boys very well, and it isn't as if I'll be alone. She's eighteen years old, and she and Ramon are as good chaperons as anyone." She had rehearsed all her answers over and over again in her mind, yet her voice ended up high and nervous.

"You are not going out alone with any boys that I have never met nor heard of. That is final! How can you even consider such a thing? I'm so shocked I don't know what to say!" Her mother had put down the piece of embroidery she was working on, and sitting erect in her chair, her mouth set firmly, and her eyes flashing, she eyed her daughter with a look that was familiar to Felicidad. It meant that her mother was not going to change her mind. All the signals showed that she was going to stick to her guns and that she was on the warpath. Felicidad felt, with a sinking heart, that the battle would be a losing one for her.

Pleadingly she looked at Mrs. Esteves for help, but Mrs. Esteves shook her head and said, "I'd better stay out of this. I know how your mother feels, and I am sick in my heart at the way Margarita runs around. But at least I know she's with Carlos, and I've known Carlos since he was born. That makes a difference."

"But, Mama, you can't keep me from going out," Felicidad said helplessly. "What am I supposed to do? Just sit here in the kitchen with you every night?" Frustration was welling up within her. "I've been dying to come to New York, and now you want me to stay in here like a stick or like a baby hanging on to its mother's apron. If you went out and met more people yourself, you'd know what it's like. Everything's different here!"

"I don't care for the difference." Her mother drew herself up even straighter. "I want to bring you up the way I was brought up, like a good Spanish girl. Not like up here."

"But that's impossible!" Felicidad wailed. "We *are* up here. You're not in Spain, and we're not in Puerto Rico!" She didn't want to lose her temper, but her frustration was turning into anger. "You're too stuck-up. You think your way is the only way and the best! You don't want to learn anything new! But you can't stop me. I'm going out with Carmen and her friends tomorrow night. And what's more, I'm going home to sleep at Carmen's house."

Felicidad stared at her mother defiantly. She had never spoken to her this way before in her life, and she was astonished at her own courage.

Her mother was white and almost speechless. "You should bite out your tongue. You deserve a good spanking," she finally said. "If that is how they teach you to behave in *Neuva York*, you'd be better off at home. I am glad your father does not have to suffer over this."

"I'm sorry, Mother," Felicidad said. "But you don't understand, that's all."

"I understand. I understand very well, and I don't like what I understand at all."

They didn't talk about it any more. Felicidad was pained by the troubled look in her mother's eyes, but she also felt that she was right. She was young, and she had a right to enjoy herself, and her mother had to get rid of her old-fashioned ways. But to stand up to her mother this way! The very idea would have been unheard of just a few months ago.

The next evening, when she brought Carmen home, her mother was her usual calm, gracious self. She would never be discourteous to a guest in her home. Carmen was gay and vivacious, and Felicidad felt her mother couldn't help but like her. But before the girls left to meet the boys, Mrs. Marquez drew Felicidad aside. "Why aren't they coming here to call for you?" she asked anxiously.

"Because they work uptown. Carmen said it would be easier and save a lot of time if we met them there."

Her mother shook her head in bewilderment. "Save time for what?"

"Don't worry, Mother. I'll be all right. *Please* don't worry." Felicidad kissed her mother on the cheek and patted her on the arm.

"She'll be fine," Carmen added. "I'll take good care of her."

Mrs. Marquez looked far from convinced as the two girls said good-by and left.

Felicidad was terribly excited and nervous as they went to meet the two boys in the lobby of the dance hall, *El Palacio*. The fight with her mother had not been resolved, and she had taken matters into her own hands, but none the less, she was more frightened than she wanted Carmen to know. She had asked her all about the boy who would be her escort. She knew his name was David Krusky and that he worked with Ramon as a shipping clerk in some big warehouse. According to Carmen, he wasn't really handsome, but he was nice-looking and a lot of fun. Aside from Jim next door, who came and talked with her often when she did baby-sitting for Mrs. Benton, David would be the first New York boy she had met, and this would certainly be her first date.

Felicidad felt very shy when Carmen introduced the two boys to her. She said, "Hello. I'm glad to meet you," in English, but she was relieved when Ramon and Carmen continued speaking Spanish.

Even David knew a few things to say in Spanish. "That's because most of the boys I work with are Puerto Rican," he explained to Felicidad.

He was quite nice-looking, with dark-brown eyes and hair that he tried to keep flat but which had a deep wave in it anyway. He laughed a lot and turned out to be an expert dancer. Felicidad was disappointed that the place was filled almost exclusively with Puerto Ricans and Negroes from Harlem. She had hoped to see just the ordinary New Yorkers her own age out having a good time, but Carmen said that this place was the most fun to go to.

It was difficult trying to keep up a conversation with David, because of the language barrier. Ramon and Carmen were totally absorbed in each other, and Felicidad was grateful that there weren't long waits between the dances. The band was excellent, and the place was very noisy and gay. Ramon ordered highballs for all of them, but Felicidad asked for plain ginger ale.

It was very late when they left, but Ramon said he was going to take them out for a little drive in his car. He took them across town and over to the West Side Highway. Felicidad had never been there before, and she thought it was perfectly beautiful, with the lights twinkling across from the Palisades and the bright winter moonlight on the Hudson River. The city seemed very quiet at this hour, and Felicidad wondered about all the people sound asleep in the tall apartment buildings that they flashed by. Were there girls her age sleeping behind those windows? What were they like? What did they think about? Did they know that there was a separate world of Spanish-speaking people right in the middle of their city?

No one seemed to pay any attention. How could you meet these other girls? She saw them going by on the streets, often laughing with each other and talking away in their unpronounceable language. They hardly looked at her, but she longed to meet and to talk with them.

The air smelled different now, and Felicidad thought they were in the country—the country or possibly a big park—because there were trees around.

Ramon pulled into a little side road and finally stopped the car in a spot overlooking a beautiful dam, where the water was spilling over the top into a lake.

"It is a reservoir for water," Ramon explained over his shoulder to Felicidad. Then, without a word, Carmen cuddled up in Ramon's arms, and Ramon's head bent over hers in a long, silent kiss.

Felicidad's heart was beating nervously. She didn't know what to do or to say. Instinctively she moved over to her side of the car, away from David, but he moved with her. She held herself tense as she felt his arm reach out around her shoulders. Uneasily she thought of her mother and of how shocked she would be by the four of them, sitting here alone in the dark this way! She was afraid to look at David, and she didn't want to look at Carmen and Ramon. She didn't know where to look or what to do. . . .

"Don't be scared," David said softly in English. But the next thing she knew, his arms were tight around her, and his lips were pressing against hers. She pushed him away with both hands, struggling to get free of his hold.

"Say, what kind of a way to act is that!" David said in astonishment.

Felicidad spoke to him indignantly in Spanish. "You cannot do such a thing to me. I am not that kind of a girl. How dare you act this way!" she ended up breathlessly.

"Calm down," David said. He tried to put his arm through hers, but Felicidad pushed him away. "What's the matter with you?" David asked her, pronouncing every word carefully so that she would understand him. "I thought all you Latin girls were supposed to be real hot stuff."

"Hot stuff?" She looked at him in bewilderment, and then she caught on. "You have the wrong idea," she told him, saying the words as well as she could in English. "All Puerto Rican girls are not alike. Some one way, some another. I do not like to kiss boys I do not know."

"But you know me," David said coaxingly.

Felicidad allowed herself to smile a little. "I don't know you. I thought all New York boys had good manners."

"Nuts!" She did not understand his exclamation, but by the tone of his voice, she thought it was just as well.

"You kiss every girl you meet?" she asked him.

"I don't often meet girls as pretty as you," he said promptly. "Besides, I did think you girls were different."

"Why are we different?" Felicidad asked impatiently. "You lump all Puerto Ricans together. Sure, we're different; we're different from each other. And our manners are better than yours—we don't kiss so easily, the way you do." David glanced in front at Carmen and Ramon, who were very obviously kissing. "They are following New York ways—not Puerto Rican," she said primly.

"But you're the ones who are supposed to be so

passionate," David said, shaking his head. "I don't get it."

"I believe you have all the wrong ideas about Puerto Ricans," Felicidad said. "Just the things you read in the newspapers. But you don't really know them at all."

"I'm trying to get to know you, but you won't let me," said David. He sat on his side of the seat disconsolately.

Felicidad felt ill at ease. She didn't know how to talk to him because of her English, and besides, she couldn't think of anything to say. She wished desperately that she was safe at home with her mother and Señora Esteves.

She was greatly relieved when Ramon and Carmen pulled apart and Ramon started up the car again and they headed for home. David still kept to his side of the car, staring out of the window indifferently. Felicidad was miserable. She felt lost and unhappy at the way the evening had ended. She felt as if every time she tried to be friendly with the people around her and to get to know some of the young people her own age, her path was blocked by a big iron door, closed in her face. Was her mother right? Was it really impossible to become an *americano?*

Her mind turned to Jim Duncan. He, too, drew a curtain down on his friendliness. He would come in and talk to her when she was baby-sitting for his aunt. They'd play records and dance or watch television, and he would talk and act as if he really liked her. But he never asked her for a date. He talked freely about all the places he went to—the parties, the movies—and about the many different times he went dancing. By now she knew each band leader by name, but it was as if he was talking to a stuffed doll, not to a girl with a heart and feelings, who had legs to dance with and a mind to understand.

Felicidad sat in her corner of the car, wrapped in her own thoughts. She was surprised when they stopped in front of Carmen's house. David said good-by to her sullenly, while Carmen gave Ramon a final good-night kiss.

Carmen's house did not make Felicidad feel any better. If this was exciting, glamorous Harlem, Felicidad didn't want any part of it. This house was even worse than hers. Carmen led her up four long flights of stairs, and the filth and garbage that were standing in the halls made the girls cover up their noses with their handkerchiefs. There were big, gaping holes in the walls, and Felicidad wondered if the house would stand up overnight.

Everyone was asleep in Carmen's apartment. Felicidad had never seen so many people sleeping together as there were in the one room they went through to get to Carmen's. There she crawled into the same narrow bed as Carmen and her three younger sisters, who were all tossing restlessly.

Carmen seemed to take it all for granted, and Felicidad felt a warm surge of affection for her friend. How could she come out of this hole looking so attractive all the time and acting so gay and full of fun? Felicidad felt both a wave of anger and a sense of pride—anger that Carmen had to live in a place like this and pride in the way she took it. How little she let it dampen her good spirits!

Felicidad's last drowsy thoughts were of Fernando. What would he have thought of her tonight? Tomorrow she would have to go to confession. There was much to talk about!

Chapter 11

⚜

A short while after Felicidad's unhappy experience with David she baby-sat again for Mrs. Benton, and Jim's familiar rap-rap came on the door.

Felicidad had been fairly sure he would come in to see her that evening, so she had dressed carefully for the occasion. She didn't have many clothes to choose from, but she wore the mustard wool skirt she had bought on her first shopping expedition in New York and a dressy blue-satin blouse she had seen in a shop window and had fallen in love with. She wore the beads Pilarín had given her as a going-away present and a pair of bright, dangling earrings.

"Hi, *señorita*," Jim greeted her in his usual friendly fashion.

"Hello, *señor*," Felicidad answered him. He had on an open-necked sports shirt, a pair of sun tans, and the sneakers that he wore even on the coldest days. Felicidad never ceased to marvel at the way Jim dressed in such cold weather. He never wore a hat or cap, and often he would go out in just a jacket or a sweater instead of a coat. "Don't you freeze?" she asked him.

"Of course not. I guess we northerners are the ones who are hot-blooded. You Latins are just fakes!"

"Everyone has such crazy ideas about Latin Americans." Felicidad lapsed into Spanish, which Jim now understood fairly well. "You think we are all passionate, that we are all what you call hot-blooded. Why should we be all alike? Do you think it is possible?"

"I guess not," Jim said, sitting on the floor, his favorite spot. "But there are such things as racial and national characteristics."

"How would you like it if I were to say all the people in the United States were cold, unfriendly, and busy with themselves, that they had foolish prejudices? It would not make much sense, would it?"

"The United States is a big country!"

"And Latin America—that is small, do you think?"

Jim laughed. "You're too smart for me. How can a girl be so smart and so pretty too? You look as if you shouldn't have to think of anything more important than which boy friend to pick."

"Would you like me better if I were stupid?" Felicidad asked him.

Jim looked up and held her eyes with his own. "I like you very much the way you are," he said, his voice suddenly serious. "You know how much I like you, don't you?"

Felicidad laughed lightly, but her heart was beating nervously. "How would I know?"

"Because you aren't that dumb, that's why," Jim said, laughing again. "How's your love life? Who's your latest conquest?"

Felicidad shook her head. "I make no conquest. Who can I conquer?"

"Oh, I see a million boys on this block—all those good-looking Puerto Ricans. I bet they're all after you."

Felicidad felt uneasy at the turn the conversation was taking. "I don't know any of them," she said quietly. "I don't go out with boys I see on the street."

"Whom do you go out with?" Jim asked.

She shrugged her shoulders. "I don't go out very much. Sometimes my girl friend and I go out together."

"But with a face and a figure like yours! Holy smoke! I thought the fellows would be tearing the doors down to get to you."

"There aren't many places for me to meet boys—that is, boys I'd care to go out with."

"I guess it is hard when you're a stranger in the city," Jim said. He changed the subject abruptly. "I've got different troubles. We have a big dance coming up at school, and I can't decide who to ask. You see, there are a couple of girls I've been going with, and if I ask one, it's going to be *finis* with the other. I can't make up my mind which one I want to keep and which one I want to let go."

"Which one do you like better?" Felicidad asked. Her eyes were on him calmly, but she could feel resentment stirring within her. He didn't care about her one bit! He spoke to her as if she didn't exist as a girl, and as if only the rough-looking boys who played out on the street were possible friends for her.

"That's the trouble. I don't know which. There's Peggy Taylor. She's real cute and a swell dancer and all that, but she's not so good on conversation. As a matter of fact, I think she's probably a little on the dumb side—well, not dumb exactly, but not too bright. And then there's Kathy Perkins. She's one of those cool blondes. You never know what's going on in her brain, but she's as smart as she can be. I don't know, though, if she really likes me or if she just wants to go out."

"You don't seem to know which one you really like yourself. Why don't you ask a third girl?"

Jim looked at her in astonishment. "Hey, that's an idea! Why didn't I think of that? That would fool them both, and I bet they'd both still go out with me anyway." Then his face fell again. "But who'd I ask? There are some girls around, but I don't know any I care about that much."

Felicidad dropped her eyes away from his face. She could feel herself getting so angry that she didn't think she could bear to go on talking to him.

He must have caught something in her face, because he suddenly became very quiet for a minute, and then he said in a funny voice, "Boy, Felicidad! I'm a fool, aren't I?"

She glanced up at him for a second, and she felt her mouth quiver unhappily. "No, you're not a fool, Jimmy," she said in a low voice.

"But Felicidad, I couldn't take you to this dance!" He ran his hand through his hair nervously. "I just couldn't. I don't know how to explain it to you. . . . My mother would have a fit . . . and you wouldn't know anyone there. . . . I'd be afraid you'd have a rotten time. . . ."

"You don't have to explain anything," Felicidad said, finally looking at him directly. She was determined to control all her mixed emotions of anger, hurt, and pride. She even felt a certain sympathy toward him, sensing in him a kind of helpless innocence.

"Doggone, it's not my fault people feel the way they do—I didn't do it. I like you—you know that—and my aunt and uncle think you're tops. For Pete's sake, they wouldn't let you stay here with Freddie if they didn't! My mother doesn't have much sense about things like this. She thinks she's better than anyone else anyway."

"I understand. My mother feels the same way," Felicidad said.

Jim looked surprised, but he didn't say anything. He stood up, embarrassed. "I guess I'd better be going," he said awkwardly. "Thanks for the advice, anyway."

When the door closed behind him, Felicidad sat

quietly with her eyes blinking. Determined not to cry, she got up and turned on the television set. The screen displayed a group of young girls and boys dancing gaily. It was too much for her to watch. With the music blaring against her ears, she buried her head in her arms and let herself give way to the sobs she'd been holding back.

They were sobs of anger as well as hurt and bewilderment. She felt like someone who belonged nowhere. She felt neither American nor Puerto Rican nor Spanish—not *anything!* Life was unfair. Those terrible doors were constantly being closed in her face! Why couldn't she be carefree and gay like Carmen? She knew that Carmen, too, sometimes got angry, but she was cynical and said it didn't bother her.

Felicidad didn't even hear the door open when the Bentons came in. She hadn't expected them home this early, and she was startled by Mrs. Benton's voice. "Felicidad, what on earth is the matter? What happened?" Mrs. Benton was bending over her anxiously.

Felicidad kept her tear-stained face covered. "It's nothing. Nothing happened. Freddie is O.K."

"I'm sure Freddie's O.K. But what about you?" Mrs. Benton motioned to her husband to go out and leave them alone. She sat down beside Felicidad and patted her gently on the shoulder. "Wouldn't you like to talk about it, Felicidad?"

"There is nothing to talk about." Felicidad still kept

her head down. She was able to speak with Mrs. Benton in English now, because Mrs. Benton spoke slowly and carefully so that she could understand. Felicidad had got over her shyness at speaking English with her. If she made a mistake she knew Mrs. Benton wouldn't laugh at her. It was easier to speak English with someone who was kind and whom you liked anyway.

"You wouldn't be crying that way over nothing. Perhaps I can help you."

"No one can help me. I should have been born in a different place. I wish we had never come to New York. I don't like it here."

"Why, Felicidad! I thought you loved New York. You seem to get along so well. Has someone been unkind to you?"

Felicidad sat up now and wiped her face with her handkerchief. "Unkind? What does that mean—unkind?"

"Not nice. Has someone been mean to you?"

Felicidad shook her head. "Not mean. But no one is very nice. In New York the people hate us, and I hate them."

"But you've said many times that all Puerto Ricans are not alike, so you can't hate all New Yorkers. They're not all alike either."

"They are alike in one thing. They hate us."

"That's not true. I don't hate you; I like you very much. Besides, what is a New Yorker? New York is made up of all different kinds of people. I'd like to take you out one day and show you. There's one section where mostly Italians live, and in Chinatown, the Chinese people live. And you know that up in Harlem there are Negroes and Puerto Ricans too. They're all New Yorkers. What do you have against all of them?"

"Nothing. I have nothing against *them*. I feel only against the people when I go to look for a job. They ask, 'Are you Puerto Rican?' And I say 'Yes,' and they have no job for me. I would like to meet girls and boys from New York, but there is no place I can meet them. I came up here, because I wanted so much to be a real New Yorker, but they say, 'You are Puerto Rican. You stay away.' It makes me feel sorry I am Puerto Rican."

"You must never be sorry for that," Mrs. Benton said emphatically. "You should be proud you are a Puerto Rican. You come from a beautiful little island, and you must never let anyone make you feel ashamed. There are difficulties—I admit that. But it's mainly lack of understanding. For instance, there are many things I don't understand about you, and sometimes, I admit, they make me a little—well, not angry—but annoyed. Do you mind if I ask you something? Please! I'm not scolding you, and I don't want to hurt your feelings; it's just something I want to know."

"What is it?" Felicidad asked.

"Well, ever since you've been coming here, I've asked you to write down telephone messages. Every time I go out I tell you, and you nod your head and say yes, and yet you have never taken a message all the time you've been here. My friends have told me they've phoned, but that you just say, 'No one home,' and hang up the receiver. We don't understand something like that. I know you must have known what I meant."

"I didn't really understand what you meant," Felicidad said earnestly.

"Then why didn't you ask me? I'd explain it to you. Why do you always say yes, even when you don't understand?"

Felicidad shrugged her shoulders. "It seems more polite. I don't like to ask you questions, so I say yes. And anyway, when the phone rings I get nervous, and I don't understand so easily how people speak, so I just say no one is home. It seems best to me. I don't like to ask them questions either."

Mrs. Benton sighed. "You see, it is all misunderstanding. When we travel, we're not shy about asking all the questions in the world, and we don't understand your kind of reticence. So you see, many New Yorkers would think what you did is foolish, or that you were lying. It's all very difficult."

"But how could I be a one-hundred-percent New Yorker? I would like to be very much."

"You stay the way you are," Mrs. Benton said. "But perhaps I can help you a little. You don't mind if I'm frank with you, do you?"

Felicidad shook her head. She wasn't sure what frank meant, but she trusted Mrs. Benton.

Mrs. Benton looked at her thoughtfully. "Clothes are very important for one thing. Now that blouse you are wearing is lovely, but a good satin blouse doesn't go with a wool sports skirt. You should wear a sweater or a tailored shirt with that. And if you wear beads, then you don't need earrings. You see, wearing the two together cheapens both of them. You don't mind my telling you these things, do you? In Puerto Rico you all look so lovely, but up here—well, I guess the clothes are different!"

"Here we want to look like New York. But I haven't got a sweater, so I wore this." Felicidad looked bewildered.

"Of course. Now wait a minute. I think I have one that's too small for me, and it would be just right for you!" She ran inside and came back with a beautiful dark-green sweater that she held up to Felicidad. "That's perfect. It's lovely with your coloring, and fine with that skirt. Please take it."

My mother wouldn't like me to take it. Felicidad thought intuitively, but she didn't want to hurt Mrs. Benton's feelings either. "Thank you very much," she said impulsively.

"Cheer up. Life isn't so bad." Mrs. Benton smiled at her. "When is your day off? I'm going to find someone else to take care of Freddie for a day, and you and I will go on a tour of New York. There's so much I'd love to show you."

"My day off is Monday," Felicidad said shyly.

"Good! Then it's a date for next Monday."

Mrs. Benton's kindness moved Felicidad enormously; yet when she said good night and left to go home, she glanced up at the light where she imagined Jimmy's room to be, and she felt a pang in her heart. Why couldn't he have been as kind as his aunt and want to be helpful?

But even Mrs. Benton's kindness seemed a great weight on her as she climbed the stairs on her way home. She tucked the green sweater under her jacket, because she didn't want her mother or Mrs. Esteves to see it. They would ask a lot of questions that she didn't feel like answering. She also felt a certain shame and a sense of betrayal in having accepted it, and once she was inside the kitchen and had stuck the sweater away in her own room, she studied herself carefully in the cracked kitchen mirror. Mrs. Benton was wrong! That blue-satin blouse was pretty, and she loved it!

She was all mixed up about how she felt about Mrs. Benton anyway. She liked her very much, yes, and she felt Mrs. Benton really wanted to be her friend, but Mrs. Benton couldn't be a real girl friend, like someone her own age. And besides, there were other things that made her feel uneasy. There was often an apologetic look in Mrs. Benton's eyes that seemed to say, "I am so sorry you are treated this way in my city, and I hope you understand that I feel different."

Felicidad *did* understand, but understanding didn't necessarily make you feel better. And no matter how nice one person was, you couldn't help but realize that for each nice person there were many, many of the others—like Mrs. Benton's own sister, Jim's mother!

And Jim. How did he *really* feel about her?

Things up here got so complicated! You felt that no one ever really liked you or disliked you for what you were. They either wanted to be kind, because you were a Puerto Rican, or they hated you, because you were a Puerto Rican! But who really cared about *her*, Felicidad Louisa Marquez?

Chapter 12

The very day that Felicidad spent with Mrs. Benton
was the day the tragedy took place.

They had had a lovely time. Mrs. Benton took her
up to Radio City Music Hall first. She said she'd never
been to the movies in the morning in her entire life,
but that she'd always been curious about it and that
this was as good a time as any to find out what it was
like. Felicidad thought it was odd going to the movies
in the morning, and she was amazed by all the people
standing in line to get in.

"Don't they have to go to work?" she asked Mrs.
Benton in astonishment.

"I guess some of them work on late shifts, or they're
out of jobs, or they just don't work at all. Remember,
New York's a big place, with all kinds of people in it."

Felicidad thought the Music Hall was perfectly beautiful. The seats were so comfortable she almost fell
asleep. When they came out she couldn't believe it

wasn't twelve o'clock yet, and she felt all mixed up about time for the rest of the day.

Mrs. Benton showed her Times Square and Broadway, and she wanted to take her up to the top of the Empire State Building, but Felicidad was afraid of the elevators shooting up so high. Instead, they went down to Chinatown for lunch. Felicidad liked this part of the day best of all. She enjoyed walking around the narrow, cobbled streets and peering into the many shop windows, where exciting ornamental oddities were on display. There were old, solemn-faced men with pigtails, sitting in the doorways, and small buildings, closed to the street, where balconies rustled emptily in the cold winter wind. The shuttered windows hinted of mysteries and of life taking place behind their anonymity. It all reminded her of the old section of San Juan back home, with its own narrow streets and teeming life, where the tourists came to look and to buy, but never saw anything beyond the shop fronts.

Felicidad felt a kinship with these soft-spoken, smooth-cheeked people, who jabbered away privately in their own tongue, who spoke so politely in English to the white lady, Mrs. Benton, but whose expressions altered a tiny bit when they looked at her with a smile. They are strangers here too, she thought, living their own closed-in lives.

Later they walked down Mulberry Street and in and out of tiny side streets, buying delicious Italian pastries and crazily shaped Italian breads, covered with sesame seeds. They went down to Grand Street, where Mrs. Benton bought Jewish delicacies. Finally, with their arms loaded, they went home in a taxi.

"Who knows what a typical New Yorker is?" she said to Felicidad. "You see, the city is made up of many different groups. Some other time I'll take you uptown to Central Park and Fifth Avenue, and I'll show you the museums and the U. N. building. And Manhattan is just a small part of New York. There are still the four other boroughs."

"There is so much to see and to learn," Felicidad said wistfully. She was very grateful to Mrs. Benton for having taken her out, and she thanked her sincerely from the bottom of her heart. And yet it did not quite satisfy the discontent within her.

She had been aware of quick, averted glances toward the well-dressed Continental lady who was escorting the Puerto Rican girl about. People had looked at them kindly, and yet there had been another look in the eyes of some of the girls her own age—in the eyes of a Chinese girl and some Negro and Italian young people. "You're not fooling us," their eyes said. "You're a Puerto Rican kid, and you're like us. She may be as nice to you as all get-out, but you'll only be welcome in your own neighborhood, with your own kind. Don't trust any of them," their flashing eyes warned.

Now she said good-by to Mrs. Benton and climbed

up her own stairs. It wasn't until later that she remembered how odd the street outside had been. It had been extremely quiet, with only a few women huddled near their baby carriages in the small patch of sunlight, but with no noisy children playing. Policemen had been everywhere, one of them breaking up a silent group of boys and telling them to go home.

The minute she walked into the kitchen, alarm hit her. There was fright and worry on the faces of her mother and Mrs. Esteves, and even Willy's dark face was strained and pale.

"What's the matter? What happened?" Felicidad turned from one of them to the other.

"There's been a stabbing over on Ninth Avenue. Two boys are dying," Mrs. Esteves told her in a toneless voice.

"But no one that we know?" Felicidad asked hurriedly. "Nothing's happened to anyone here, any of us, has it?"

"None of us has been hurt, if that's what you mean, but a terrible thing has happened to all of us. It's the Puerto Rican boys again. Now a great, new hate wave will start. The cops are rounding up every kid they can lay their hands on, and they're coming around and questioning everyone. And two young boys are dying. What difference does it make what family they come from?"

"They won't even let me go down to see Danny,"

Willy cried out indignantly. "What can happen to me right here in this house?"

"You're not going anywhere. You'll go to school and come home, and that's all." His mother spoke emphatically.

"You can't lock me up. You can't keep me in prison!" Willy was outraged.

"And you too, Felicidad," her mother said, ignoring Willy's protests. "You'll go to work and come home right afterward. I worry myself to death anyway, until you come home at night. This is no safe place to live."

"No place is safe," Mrs. Esteves said angrily. "And we Puerto Ricans get it both ways. We get blamed for some wild, crazy boys who should be in jail, and we have to live where they can get away with it. There are never any cops around, no lights on the streets, no place for the kids to play, and nothing for them to do but have these crazy gangs! What can they expect? I'm not excusing these terrible boys who stab innocent kids, but there'll always be trouble when you have to live like this and bring up your children like this."

The others were quiet. They knew that what she said was true. Willy sullenly swatted at a roach crawling up the wall.

"If they killed the rats and the *cucarachas,* it would be better," Mrs. Esteves added, grabbing up a can of insecticide and spraying the walls furiously.

"And Willy won't tell me where he was this afternoon," Mrs. Marquez said, breaking her gloomy silence. "He came home just a little before you did, Felicidad, running so hard he couldn't get his breath, and I can't get a word out of him. Maybe he'll tell you."

Felicidad felt terror, as a stony mask dropped over Willy's small, childish face. "I didn't go no place," he muttered, and stalked out of the kitchen and into the bedroom he shared with Carlos. The two women and Felicidad heard the door slam behind him.

Mrs. Marquez was in tears. "My children weren't like this at home. Carlos, you, and now my baby, slamming doors, being insolent and rude. Felicidad, go and talk to him. I'm worried sick about that child."

"Mama, he was probably just playing with Danny and afraid to tell you." Mrs. Marquez had still never befriended Willy's favorite playmate.

"No, he wasn't. Danny came up looking for him, and then he played right in the hall here, waiting for Willy to come home. I sent him downstairs just a few minutes before Willy got back. He made me nervous out in the hall there—probably eavesdropping. Heaven knows what he was doing!"

"Oh Mama!" was all Felicidad could answer, but she did follow Willy into his room.

The boy was sitting on the three-quarter-size bed, which practically took up the entire room. He was huddled up and looked small and frightened, a very different boy from the one who had been defying his mother only a few minutes before. He was staring out the window, but the scene outside was bleak. Whatever little sunshine sometimes filtered through was gone by late afternoon. What he looked at was a solid brick wall on two sides, and facing him, the unwashed windows of apartments like his own—overcrowded, with eight and ten people living in one room, and the houses tragically in need of repair. The small courtyard below was littered with debris and garbage.

His face was both sullen and worried. "What is the matter, Willy?" Felicidad asked, softly closing the door behind her. "Where were you this afternoon?"

"No place," he said. But then after a few minutes of silence he mumbled, "I was hiding."

"Hiding? What for?" Felicidad knew from experience that if she waited long enough, Willy would tell her everything.

"Promise you won't tell anybody?" Willy's eyes were pleading. "Most of all Mama. I'll kill you if you tell her!"

"I promise," Felicidad said.

"There's a gang around here, the Black Arrows, and they don't want me to have anything to do with Danny. They call him a dirty nigger, and they say they're going to get every nigger in the neighborhood."

Felicidad was shocked. Willy's face was so frightened

that small shivers raced up and down her spine. "What kind of boys are in the gang, Willy?" she asked, but she knew his answer before he gave it.

"Mostly Puerto Rican kids," he said resignedly. "Most of them don't want to be in it, but there's a couple of guys that make them. They're scared not to."

"Are you in it, Willy?" Felicidad looked directly into her younger brother's eyes, until Willy was forced to pull his away.

"Yes and no," he finally said. "I have one of their shirts, but I don't want Mama to see it. I wear it when I get away from here. They don't let me go to any of their meetings, but they've given me warnings about Danny. Want to see the shirt?"

Felicidad nodded her head. Willy lifted up the mattress and pulled a white, long-sleeved, cotton shirt from under it. Down the center of the back it had a long, slender, black arrow woven into it, reaching from the collarless neck to the hem. The arrow gave it a menacing, sinister look—like a snake—that terrified Felicidad. She didn't want to touch the shirt for fear it would come to life.

"Put it away! Put it back!" she said hastily, glancing nervously at the door. If their mother came in and saw that, there was no telling what she might say. "Oh Willy, what are you going to do?" Felicidad turned to him in distress.

Willy shrugged his shoulders. "I dunno. I'm scared."

"I think we ought to tell Carlos," Felicidad said hopefully. "He'll know what to do."

"What can he do? And you promised! Carlos'll tell Mama, and . . . I don't know what *she'll* do!"

"Carlos won't tell Mama. Please let me tell him. We must."

Willy shrugged again, helplessly. "I don't care. Tell him if you want, but it won't do any good. I know." His face was hopeless. "You don't know those guys," he added.

"If you know anything you should go and tell the police," Felicidad said.

"The cops? You think I'm crazy? I wouldn't go near them for anything!" Willy looked at her in disgust.

"Why did you want to see Danny? Hadn't you better keep away from him?"

"Yeah, I guess so. But I wanted to go down and tell him. I've got to see him for a few minutes. Only Mama wouldn't let me."

"Run down now. I'll tell Mama you went to get me something at the store. But be quick about it, Willy. And Willy," she added in a gentler voice, "don't hurt Danny's feelings. Tell him it's not the way you feel about him, but that it'll just be safer to stay away from him for a little while now."

"O.K.," Willy said in English, giving Felicidad a grateful look.

Before joining the women in the kitchen, Felicidad sat in the boys' room for a while, trying to digest what Willy had told her. Mrs. Esteves was right. There'd be a new hate wave against the Puerto Ricans now, just because of a few boys who were so desperate with hate themselves that they took their hate out on the nearest scapegoat, the minority of Negroes in the neighborhood. And whom did the Negroes hate? It was a vicious circle that seemed to have no end.

That night Felicidad pretended to go to bed as usual, but she didn't go to sleep. She lay awake, waiting to hear Carlos and Margarita come in. The minute she heard the door open, she slipped on her robe and went into the kitchen.

As Felicidad told her story, Margarita huddled close to Carlos, her eyes getting wider by the minute. Carlos sat silent, listening, the expression on his face solemn.

"We heard about the stabbing," he said soberly, when she'd finished. "This whole neighborhood is like a funeral parlor. Are you sure Willy was telling the truth?"

Felicidad's heart fluttered nervously. "I'm sure," she said sincerely. "He wasn't making anything up. Don't you think he should talk to the police?"

Carlos' face took on the same expression of disgust as Willy's. "What good will that do? He's got nothing to tell them, and he'd better not get mixed up with them."

"But what else can he do?"

"Nothing," Carlos said flatly. "Tell him just to do what Mama says, to go to school and come right home. And to keep away from that Danny kid! We'll just have to sit tight and hope it all blows over. It will, I suppose."

"Do you think the police will find the boys who did the stabbing?" Margarita asked Carlos. She looked at him as if he had all the answers.

"I doubt it. They don't stand much of a chance around here. Those guys are well-protected, and everyone clams up. They all get scared. No one's going to talk to the cops."

"Oh, Carlos, I hope they don't come after you!" Margarita pressed his arm close to her.

"Don't worry about me. I can take care of myself. They won't bother me anyway." Carlos spoke reassuringly, but the two girls exchanged swift glances of apprehension.

"Go to bed, Felicidad," Carlos said. "And don't you go out anyplace at night. Come right home from work. Do you understand?"

"O.K.," Felicidad said, and she went into the cold bed, hoping Margarita would come in soon to keep her warm. Tonight it would be especially comforting to have her close by.

Chapter 13

Carlos was right. There was a funereal pall over the entire neighborhood. People stayed off the street as much as possible. Children went right home from school. Women didn't stop to gossip on the street; they did their marketing at the stores and came home quickly. The younger women kept their babies indoors, and the men went to work quietly and hurried to return home before dark if they could. The police broke up any groups of boys they saw gathering.

Prayers were said in the churches for the two young boys who died, and the people prayed for a better understanding in the beautiful big city they had come to with so much hope. They were torn between shame for the vicious criminals who had done the stabbing, and resentment against those who cried out, "The Puerto Ricans are ruining our city!" They knew they had some bad elements, but perhaps fewer than many other groups, and they also knew that no matter how hard they tried, they were at a disadvantage. So many of the fine things the city had to offer were not for them. They did not live in the beautiful new apartments on the wide avenues; the really good job opportunities were not for them; they had no new schools and playgrounds; and for most of them, the money they earned was far less than that of the average New Yorker.

Felicidad was filled with worry and resentment. Nothing was turning out as she had dreamed it would. At home she had loved reading the beautiful magazines from the States, especially those written for the teenager, and she had imagined life in New York from the gaily colored photographs. She had seen herself wearing all those lovely clothes, with a handsome Continental boy by her side, going out dancing, visiting all the exciting places that she read about, and going to the theaters and concerts or walking up Fifth Avenue to Central Park. She had imagined herself smartly dressed and perhaps being a secretary in an office or working in one of the fine stores. They would be living in an apartment house with a little elevator that went up and down, and one of those beautiful tiled bathrooms she saw in the ads, while her mother, pretty like the women in the pictures, had a sparkling kitchen with a fine stove and refrigerator. She had dreamed of Carlos' making a lot of money and of Willy's finding suitable friends—boys who would be a good influence and encourage him to go on to college and choose a good profession.

It was all a dream.

Felicidad let out her anger everywhere that was near and handy. She began to hate her job more each day. She felt sorry for Mr. Marin. He worked hard to make both ends meet, but only Puerto Ricans would come to his restaurant, and none of them could afford to spend much money, so he had to cut down every way he could. As a result, the three girls who worked there had to do the work of six, and sometimes in the rush hour Felicidad felt as if she wanted to throw the food at the customers.

Of course she didn't do that, but it got so that she cared less and less about being efficient, because all she could think of was hurrying. Since most of the customers were poor, the tips were few and far between, and there seemed to be no incentive to do a good job. The smells from the food often made her feel sick, and even the cook's bright smile and good humor failed to cheer her up.

"You're getting the disease of the Puerto Ricans," the cook said to her one day. "The I-don't-care attitude. That's no good. You mustn't let it happen to you. You're too smart a girl for that."

"Well, I don't blame them if they don't care," Felicidad said wearily. "But don't worry about me. I'm all right."

But his words bothered her. She knew she wasn't all right. She had become careless about going to church.

She never confided in her mother any more, and, too often for her own comfort, she heard herself saying to her, "You don't know what you're talking about. You don't understand!"

The whole atmosphere at home and in the neighborhood was getting on her nerves. She was worried sick about Willy, and even Mrs. Benton's kindness seemed more than she could bear. Why should Mrs. Benton *have* to be kind to her?

Felicidad found herself doing foolish little things that she despised herself for later. She still hung up the phone on Mrs. Benton's friends; she threw paper on the streets, because she hated the dirt that was already there; she got lazy about scrubbing her room at home. What was the use of any of it, when life was just working and coming home to go to sleep, and everything around you was dirty to start with?

The only excitement in her life at all was seeing Jim, and that was certainly a very mixed-up problem for her. Now that she didn't go out at all, not even with Carmen and her friends, she had as many evenings free to stay with Freddie as Mrs. Benton wanted. So she found herself there three or four nights a week, and very often Jim would come in to spend some of the time with her.

When he was with her, she felt that he was the most wonderful person in the world. They had progressed enough so that they could talk about most things, and

Jim was very sympathetic and understanding since the tragic stabbings. It seemed as if he really wanted to go out of his way to make her understand that he did not hold it against her people. They talked about it at great length.

"All you Puerto Ricans seem to be gay and having fun all the time," Jim said. "It's hard to remember that you're getting a rotten deal up here."

Felicidad laughed. "Sure we have fun. We like music; we like to dance. In our house there's always music playing. Carlos and Margarita—they dance all the time. But that doesn't mean we don't like to live in good clean houses and that we don't like the same things in life as you. We just don't cry when we can't have them."

"You get angry, though, I suppose—and I don't blame you."

"Sometimes we get angry. Or sometimes we get what the cook where I work calls the Puerto Rican disease— the I-don't-care." Felicidad shrugged her shoulders. "But we still have our fun."

Jim took her in his arms, and they danced together silently. "You're so pretty," he murmured. "I wish. . . ." His voice trailed off. Felicidad wriggled out of his arms. There was always this curtain between them. She felt as if this room of Mrs. Benton's was the only place where they could meet and be friends.

Often she imagined herself going out, laughing, on

Jim's arm, as she had seen his friends do. Groups of girls and boys were always trooping in and out of the house. They always looked as if they were having a marvelous time, and Felicidad often wondered what they would think of Jim's private Puerto Rican girl friend. It was at times like this that she listened to her mother and Mrs. Esteves talk about the stuck-up Mrs. Duncan next door, and she wondered what both her mother and Jim's mother would think if they knew they spent so much time together. Felicidad was positive his mother knew nothing about these evenings, because she had carefully noted that Jim never appeared until his parents had already gone out. And certainly her own mother knew nothing about them.

The only ones who did know were Mr. and Mrs. Benton, but this was one subject Felicidad never discussed with Mrs. Benton.

On this particular evening Jim sat down cross-legged on the floor. Then he stretched out on his stomach. Finally he got up and walked around the room restlessly. "You are like a lion in a cage tonight," Felicidad said teasingly. "What's the matter with you? Are you in love?"

Jim gave her a surprised look. "Maybe I am, and I don't know it." He ran his fingers through his blond hair nervously. "Felicidad, if I asked you to go out with me, would you come?" he asked abruptly.

Felicidad stared at him silently and then lowered her

eyes. "I don't know. I'd have to ask my mother," she said automatically. She felt stunned by the suddenness of his question. She had dreamed often of some time when he might ask her to go out with him, but by now she had felt it would never happen. And now suddenly, there he was, looking at her with such eyes—as if no one in the world existed but the two of them and that they would sit here forever staring at each other.

"Well, I'm asking you. I'd like you to go out with me next Friday night. We'll go to a restaurant I know for dinner, and we'll go out dancing. Will you come?"

Felicidad's heart hammered so excitedly that she was sure he must hear it. "I'll have to ask my mother," she said demurely, but she knew wild horses couldn't keep her from saying yes to him.

Felicidad ran home that night bursting with gaiety. The whole world had changed for her in one short evening, with a look in a boy's eyes and with one brief sentence, "Will you come out with me?" Her father always used to say that if you wanted something to happen, you must stop thinking about it. She wasn't absolutely sure she had ever stopping thinking about wanting Jim to ask to take her out—it had always been there as something to think and to dream about—but she had given up hope of its ever becoming a reality.

The warm kitchen seemed cheerful to Felicidad this night. The smell from the kerosene stove wasn't so bad, and Mrs. Esteves' printed spread, draped across the wall, looked bright. Felicidad prayed silently that her mother would be in a good mood.

Her excitement and happiness must have been shining on her face. The minute she walked in, Mrs. Esteves said, "What happened to you? You look as if you'd found a five-dollar bill on the street."

"It's better than that." Felicidad grinned. "Mama . . . Jim Duncan asked me to go out with him! Oh, isn't it wonderful!" She danced a few steps to the music coming from the radio.

Her mother's face was distressed. "My dearest, you can't go out with him unchaperoned."

"Mama dear, let's not go into that all over again. Things are different here." Felicidad took her mother's usual objections lightly.

"They are not that different. I gave in before, but that time you were going out with another couple, and other times Carlos has been with you. But to go out with this boy alone—that is impossible. His mother does not even greet me."

"Now Mama, please." Felicidad was trying hard to hold on to her wonderful mood of lightheartedness. "It's not until next week anyway—Friday night. We have plenty of time to talk about it."

"There is nothing to talk about. This time I will not change my mind." Mrs. Marquez eyed her daughter anxiously, but her voice was firm. "You will not tweedle me around."

Mr. Esteves was home from work for a change, and he laughed heartily at Mrs. Marquez's remark. "That's what you think," he said. "And that's what we used to say to Margarita. Now she always gets her own way."

Mrs. Esteves sighed. "What can one do?"

Felicidad refused to lose her mood of gaiety, but she, too, was worried about these frequent arguments with her mother. They were fights that nobody really won. Her mother would never change her mind and give her permission, but Felicidad also would not give up her rapidly changing ways.

It made her feel as if everything between herself and her mother was topsy-turvy, as if she was now becoming the grownup and her mother was turning into a child. She found herself feeling warm and tender and affectionate toward her mother, but sad that her mother was stuck in a groove she would never get out of, while Felicidad herself was learning something new every day.

Sometimes she wondered what it would be like if they went home to Barranquitas. Would they just slide back to where they had been? Felicidad didn't think so. I'll never *un*learn the new ways I've picked up here, she thought. I like them, and it makes me feel grown-up. She took a few steps, dancing in time to the radio music. I *am* grown-up, and I'm going out with Jim!

There was a soft knock on the door. "Felicidad, see who's there," her mother told her.

Felicidad opened the door and was astonished to see Mrs. Smith, Danny's mother. The woman appeared to be extremely distressed. She stood in the doorway and addressed them all, but her eyes were on Mrs. Marquez's face.

"I don't want to ask you any favors," she said with dignity, "but the police have been questioning my Danny. Somebody said a colored boy started that fighting. I told them he was here in the house that whole day when those boys got hurt, but I don't think they believe me. The social worker came to see me that day, and she didn't see him. But he says you saw him when he was up here." Her eyes finally left Mrs. Marquez's face, and she looked around at the others pleadingly.

"Only Mrs. Marquez was home. I was out that afternoon," Mrs. Esteves said gently. "Maybe the police won't come here."

The Negro woman shrugged her shoulders. "I don't know. But if they do, will she tell them?" She was asking Mrs. Esteves.

"She doesn't understand English," Mrs. Esteves said. "I'll explain it to her."

"Thank you." Mrs. Smith nodded her head and everyone sat listening to her steps going back down the stairs. Quickly Mrs. Esteves explained to Mrs. Marquez what she had wanted.

Mrs. Marquez looked frightened. "I cannot speak to the police," she said in Spanish, and she shook her head vigorously. "I don't want to have anything to do with them! I know nothing about Danny anyway. I only saw him for a minute."

"But you said he was playing right out here in the hall all afternoon. You told me that," Felicidad said.

Her mother put up her hands. "I don't know anything. I cannot talk to any policeman!"

"But Mother, you have to!" Felicidad said earnestly. "You have to tell them the truth about Danny. You don't want him to get into trouble."

"I know nothing. I don't like to talk to the policeman," her mother said firmly.

Felicidad was burning with indignation. "Mrs. Esteves, you'll have to make her. She can't do this to Danny. Will you do something?"

Mrs. Esteves tried to calm Felicidad. "Don't get excited. The police haven't come yet, and maybe they won't. Please don't get your mother upset."

"How can she act this way?" For a few minutes Felicidad was so impatient with her mother that she almost forgot her coming date with Jim. But as soon as she got into bed she started thinking about the dress she would buy for next Friday night. She'd have to save every penny. Maybe she'd be able to owe her mother the weekly amount she took out of her pay as her share of the rent and board, but she absolutely had to have a glorious new dress for her Friday-night date.

Chapter 14

Felicidad spent all of her next Monday off trying to find exactly the right dress to wear for Friday night. She went to the huge store on Fourteenth Street and walked up and down the racks examining each and every dress. She tried to judge each one by what Mrs. Benton would think of it. Would she think the color too bright? Would she consider the style too flashy? Felicidad carried them into the dressing room three at a time, because that was all the saleswoman would allow her. She tried them on, one after the other, and then she had to get dressed and come out to start all over again—another three carried off!

She couldn't decide which one looked best. Finally she narrowed her choice down to two—a beautiful black velvet with a little lace collar and a full skirt and a pale-blue satin sheath with which she could wear lots of jewelry. She thought she looked older and more sophisticated in the black velvet, and she was sure Mrs. Benton would approve of that one the most, so she finally made her purchase. Then she went down to the basement for a pair of suède shoes to go with it. On the way out she couldn't resist a choker necklace made up of four strands of pearls.

She turned toward home in the cold dusky twilight with her purchases tightly clasped in her arms. Fourteenth Street had a pink glow over it from the sun, sinking behind the Jersey marshes, and Felicidad felt a certain beauty in the city that she had never been aware of before. People were emerging from the subway entrance, pulling up their collars against the cold and stepping out briskly toward home, while others poured out of the surrounding office buildings and were swallowed up in the darkness of the underground. There was a rhythm in the movement of the flow of bodies and in the voices and sounds, which found a response in Felicidad's soft, even heartbeat. Perhaps for the first time in all the months since she had arrived, she felt a kinship with the city, a sense of the excitement, of the wonder, and of the hope that a teeming, tumultuous city can bring to a young stranger.

I have a date with Jim. . . . I have a date with Jim. . . . I am a real New York girl. . . . I am a real New York girl. This was the song the city was singing to her, and Felicidad's heart sang merrily in response.

She was radiant when she climbed up the stairs at Twentieth Street and flung her boxes on the kitchen table, eager to show her purchases to her mother and to

Mrs. Esteves. "Wait till you see what I've bought. Just wait till you see!" she cried joyfully. "I never saw such beautiful clothes anywhere."

She stopped abruptly, suddenly noticing the worried frown on Mrs. Esteves' face and the way her mother was sitting by the window, her lips pressed tightly together and her face tense and nervous. "What happened? What's the matter now?" Felicidad asked anxiously.

Mrs. Esteves let out a deep sigh. "The police were here. They wanted to ask your mother about Danny, but she locked herself in the bedroom and wouldn't come out."

Mrs. Marquez's face twitched nervously. "I can't speak to them. I can't speak English. How can I talk to them?" She turned her face back to the window.

Mrs. Esteves gave Felicidad a sympathetic glance. "I tried to get her to come out, but she wouldn't budge."

"But Mother, that's not fair! Danny was here; you *know* he was here. That's all you had to tell the police. You can say that much in English!"

"I don't want to get mixed up with any policeman. Danny told them he was playing here. They'll believe him."

"Maybe they will, and maybe they won't. It's not fair! . . . Where's Willy?" Felicidad asked suddenly.

"I wish I knew. He came home from school, and then he went out again," her mother told her.

"That's what's upsetting her. She's so worried about Willy," Mrs. Esteves said kindly. "She's afraid if she talks to the police, she'll get Willy into trouble."

"You can't get Willy into any trouble telling the police about Danny," Felicidad argued. But she, too, glanced at the clock anxiously. It was dark out now, and she wished Willy were home. With a sudden tug of fear she ran into his room, and closing the door behind her, she lifted up the corner of his mattress to see if the awful shirt was there. Her heart pumped wildly as she frantically pulled the mattress away from the springs. The springs were bare. The shirt was gone. Willy must have gone to one of those terrible meetings.

Felicidad turned cold with fear. Willy, Willy, why didn't you do as we asked you to?

She composed herself, however, before going back into the kitchen, and with an attempt at gaiety she undid the string and showed off her new clothes. She had come in feeling radiant and marvelous, loving New York, loving the world, and now she wondered where it had all disappeared to.

Couldn't anything really good happen in this city? Couldn't you feel alive and wonderful and hopeful for more than just a brief few moments?

Felicidad tried to recapture her feeling of excited expectancy as she tried on the dress and shoes and clasped the pearls around her throat to show them to her mother and Mrs. Esteves. They were extravagant in their praise, and her spirits lifted a little. But it was a familiar step running up the stairs and Willy's loud banging at the door that finally let her relax and admire herself in the spotted, cracked mirror. Willy was home, safe and sound, and one more day had been lived through.

In the course of the week, however, as Friday drew closer and closer, Felicidad's spirits soared again. Thursday night she washed and set her hair, and manicured her nails. Mrs. Esteves teased her about all her preparations, while Mrs. Marquez looked on silently and with a disapproving eye. Only once did her mother burst out—to tell her again how terrible she thought it was for her to go out alone with Jim Duncan.

Felicidad tried to soothe her as best she could, but there was nothing in the world her mother could say that would make her give up this big event. Her mind was jumping ahead. This was just the beginning. Now at last, with Jim as her escort, she could get to meet real New York boys and girls. She felt shy just thinking about it, and she examined more closely the chic business girls she saw on the streets and on the buses. She wanted to look, walk, talk, and dress just the way they did. She wanted Jim to be proud of her, and she found herself constantly daydreaming, seeing herself laughing and talking with the attractive young people she saw going in and out of Jim's house.

Fortunately Jim's younger brother had been away at school, so there was no more danger of his fighting with Willy, but he had seemed less of an ogre the past week end when he was home. Felicidad had been able to smile and say hello to him in a friendly way.

Finally Friday evening arrived. Felicidad had arranged to leave work early so she would be home and dressed and ready to meet Jim at seven o'clock. He had said he would buzz her bell and she could come down. For once she locked herself in the kitchen to take her time getting washed and only laughed at Willy's complaints at being shut up in his room. "You can wait," she called out to him. "Tonight I must make myself beautiful!"

At a quarter to seven she was all ready and waiting. Mrs. Esteves lent her a coat, so she wouldn't have to wear her short sports jacket, and said she looked exquisite. Her mother didn't make any comment, but her wide, bright, admiring eyes gave her away. Felicidad paraded back and forth around the kitchen, her heart beating nervously.

Ten minutes to seven . . . five minutes to seven . . . the bell buzzed. But it was the escaped Willy coming up from downstairs. "You look O.K., Sis," was his casual comment. But that, from Willy, was a lot.

Seven o'clock came and went, but no Jim. "He probably got home late from school," Felicidad said aloud to no one in particular. She powdered her nose for the fourth time and carefully brushed over the top of her hair to make it shiny and sleek, without disturbing it altogether.

"He'll be along. Don't worry," Mrs. Esteves said comfortingly.

"I don't know why you want to go out with that punk anyway," Willy remarked. "He's no better than his dumb brother."

"You shut your mouth," Felicidad said. "You don't know him at all."

"I know him enough to know he's stuck-up," Willy retorted.

"Oh, be quiet!" Felicidad said impatiently.

It was almost seven-thirty when the buzzer sounded. Felicidad jumped up and put on Mrs. Esteves' coat. She grabbed her bag and went to the door. Then she ran back, kissed her mother good-by, gave Mrs. Esteves an impetuous hug, and ran down the steps. Halfway down she ran into Danny, who thrust a piece of paper into her hand.

"The guy next door gave me a quarter to give you this," he said proudly. "Can you imagine—a whole quarter for that!"

Felicidad's hand, as she took the note, turned icy cold. It was too dark in the hallway to read it. Her heart beating wildly, she slowly walked over to the tiny, naked hall window that faced the street, and held up the folded piece of heavy white note paper to the light that was shining from the street lamp outside. She had never seen Jim's handwriting before. It was more like printing than writing, each letter clear and round and separate.

"Honey," she read, saying each word aloud softly to herself, "please forgive me for getting this to you so late. The truth is, I have a nasty headache and cold. I kept hoping I'd feel better, but no go. Give me a rain check, please. See you soon. Love, Jim."

Felicidad stood at the window a long time. She had seen Jim only that morning on his way to school, and he hadn't shown any signs of a cold. While she was staring out of the window a taxi drew up and let out two girls and a boy, young friends of Jim's, who ran up the steps to his house, laughing gaily. Felicidad stood dry-eyed, still staring out of the window. Across the street there were houses, just like hers, most of them with some kind of curtain at the window in a feeble attempt at privacy. But the harsh lights inside glared through. She saw Puerto Rican women in their kitchens cleaning up; she saw weary men, their elbows resting on the table, reading the newspaper with a bare bulb for light. She saw children playing, while others tried to do their homework—lots of children everywhere. From somewhere in her own house a radio blared forth with Latin-American dance music. She thought of home and of Fernando.

What was it all about, this world within a world?

She wished she could hate Jim, but it was only the cold face of his mother that filled her with a fierce bitterness. She knew she was behind this. How could people live this way, side by side on the same block, in the same city, Americans both, and yet not be allowed to reach out to each other with any real friendship?

Felicidad could not name any of the conflicting emotions racing through her being—hate, resentment, shame, hurt, wonder, indignation. All she knew was that the world was a bleak, dark place.

After a while she went back upstairs. She was silent when she came in the door. "What happened?" Mrs. Esteves exclaimed. "I thought you'd gone."

Felicidad threw the crumpled note paper into the wastebasket. "Jim's sick. He has a cold," she said in a low, lifeless voice.

Her mother looked up quickly, her eyes startled. "Oh, Baby!" She came across the room quickly and folded Felicidad into her arms. "Oh, Baby, don't care about him. He's no good!"

Her mother's quick sympathy was too much for Felicidad, and she let the sobs burning her throat escape. She buried her head against her mother's breast, as she hadn't done for many years, and cried until she was exhausted.

Mrs. Marquez stroked her hair gently, but the voice in which she denounced Jim, his mother, father, brother, and his whole family was harsh and angry.

"People like that aren't fit to live in America," she ended up emphatically. "They don't belong here. They are no good!"

Felicidad lifted her tear-stained face. "It's not just them—it's everyone," she said moodily. "It's you too, Mama—the way you feel about Danny." Felicidad suddenly sat up straighter. "Mama, why don't you go tell the police about Danny?" She looked at her pleadingly.

Suddenly she felt a tremendous urgency about Danny. Wild thoughts raced through her mind. The police could harm him unjustly! The thought of such a thing at this moment was more than she could bear. Somewhere, in a place that she could see, there must be absolute right and wrong; there must be honesty and justice somewhere; there must be no prejudice against anyone because of nationality or color.

She felt as if the Blessed Virgin were close beside her, as if perhaps she were guiding her words. She drew herself up. "Mama, you must go and tell them about Danny. Tell them he was here, playing in the hall all that afternoon. I'll go with you right now."

She felt as if somehow she must redeem the human race, that she, her mother, and all those who were close and whom she loved had to be clean and pure. She did not want the tiniest part of her mother to resemble the cold hatred of the woman next door. It was up to them to make up for her nastiness and for what her son Jim had done to Felicidad tonight.

Her mother must have sensed the depth of her daughter's emotion. She continued to stroke her hair. "If you'll come with me, I'll go," she murmured.

The police officer listened attentively to Felicidad's faltering English. She said she didn't know what they wanted of Danny but that her mother knew he'd been playing inside the house all that terrible afternoon. The policeman nodded his head and thanked them very much for coming to tell him. The whole visit took about ten minutes. But when they left the station house, Felicidad linked her arm through her mother's, and she felt a great warmth for her.

She was aware also of another feeling, a renewal of the feeling she'd had earlier that week when she'd done her shopping on Fourteenth Street, a sense of kinship with the city, a feeling of involvement, of being part of the exciting and mysterious life throbbing around her. Perhaps it was the courage it had taken to march into the austere police station to tell her mother's story. Perhaps it was the warmth and friendliness in the face of the young police officer. Or perhaps it was her first true participation in the life of New York, where, as Mrs. Benton had said, eight million people of every color, race, and religion *did* live together in spite of their differences and their misunderstandings.

They walked back home arm in arm, and Felicidad

felt there was a new lift to her mother's head too, and a relief in her eyes. Perhaps her mother also felt that the city was causing something new to flow through her veins, filling her mind with new thoughts that needed digesting.

"I'm glad we went," her mother said, squeezing Felicidad's arm affectionately. "I am not too old to learn some new ways," she added with a shy smile.

"I guess we all have something to learn up here," Felicidad said out of her newly born wisdom.

Chapter 15

⚜

The following Saturday night Margarita and Carlos persuaded Felicidad to go out with them. They'd heard about her bitter disappointment of the evening before, and they wanted to cheer her up. "We'll show you the real New York," Carlos promised gaily. "Come on."

Felicidad was touched by their concern, and she readily agreed. She had seen Jim out on the street during the day, but she had quickly stepped into a doorway in order to avoid him, because the hurt was still a conscious pain. But once again she put on her new velvet dress, her high-heeled suède shoes, and her pearl necklace.

She hadn't spent an evening like this with Margarita and Carlos for a long time, and she was looking forward to being with them, yet she was aware that she and Margarita had grown away from each other. They had been drifting their separate ways all the time Felicidad had been in New York. It was additional evi-

198

dence that the family had fallen apart, and it bothered Felicidad.

Margarita looked different from the way she had in Puerto Rico. She dressed in a much more sophisticated manner, and she was more forward with Carlos, snuggling up to him and kissing him in public—something she would never have done at home—and she never confided in Felicidad any more.

Carlos hadn't changed as much as Margarita. Perhaps he was gayer and less moody than he had been, but he still had the same little-boy quality of accepting no criticism, of being quick to flare up but eager to hurt no one.

Carlos took the girls uptown to his favorite Spanish dance hall, where they were joined by several of his and Margarita's friends. The party was a gay one, and Carlos' friends danced with Felicidad a great deal.

Felicidad had a very good time, but toward the end of the evening a funny thing happened. They were talking about where to buy clothes and what to buy, and one of the young men, just recently arrived from home in Mayagüez, was addressing Carlos.

"You are a real New Yorker. You tell me where to go," he said in Spanish.

"I know the best stores. I'll tell you everything," Carlos boasted. "I am a one-hundred-percent New Yorker!"

Felicidad looked at her brother curiously. *Was* he a

real New Yorker? She studied the rest of the group at the table and at the tables around them. They were all Puerto Rican. They were all speaking Spanish, and the store Carlos was talking about was owned by a Puerto Rican friend of his. The orchestra was playing Latin-American music, and except for a slight difference in the clothes—especially the warm jackets and coats on the backs of the chairs—there was nothing that said they were in New York!

Felicidad felt alarmed and detached by the thoughts in her head, and she had an inexpressibly strong longing to see Fernando and to be home in her beloved mountains.

No one knew what she was thinking, and everyone else seemed happy. This was what they wanted; *they wanted to be left to themselves,* even though, like Carlos, they liked to think of themselves as "New Yorkers." How foolish she had been to want anything different! She had wanted to come here and to be truly transformed into a one-hundred-percent New Yorker, as if some magic thing were going to change her.

No. She was different from a New York girl. She looked different, her temperament was different, and her language was different. And perhaps it was better to stay the way she was.

Part of the dream of belonging in this big city had been to go out with Jim Duncan. The end of that episode had now opened her eyes to the impossible foolishness of what she had been longing for. She was the girl from Puerto Rico, and she would be that wherever she went. Felicidad sat up straight, because it occurred to her at that moment that that might be a very good thing to be.

"Don't look so serious," whispered the young man who had asked her to dance. "You should laugh here. You should enjoy yourself."

"I am laughing. I am enjoying myself very much," Felicidad said, as she fell into step with him.

It was very late when they got home, and when Carlos softly turned the key in their apartment door, all three of them were startled to find the kitchen lights blazing and Mr. and Mrs. Esteves and their mother huddled around the kerosene stove.

"What happened? What's the matter?" they asked in a chorus.

Mrs. Marquez's eyes were tear-stained, and it was Mr. Esteves who spoke first. "Willy—he isn't home. We don't know where he is."

Felicidad rushed to her mother and held her close. "Have you called the police?" she asked.

Mr. Esteves shook his head. "I've begged them to tell the police," he said excitedly. "But no, they are both afraid. They're both afraid of the police!"

"I wish Father Sebastian were here." Mrs. Marquez sighed. "He'd know what to do."

"Well, he isn't here," Carlos said. "I don't like to go to the police any more than you do, but this time I'm going. Right now." He turned to the door.

His mother rushed over to him and looked pleadingly into his face. "Don't let them hurt my Willy," she said, sobbing.

Carlos gently sat her down on a chair. "Mama, the police won't hurt Willy. That's not what I'm afraid of."

Mrs. Esteves got busy serving them the inevitable *café con leche* while they waited for Carlos to return. No one spoke much. Everyone's eyes turned to the round-faced kitchen clock as it ticked away. Half-past one . . . two o'clock . . . two-fifteen. . . .

"It's such a big city," Mrs. Esteves murmured. "How can they find one little boy?"

"God wills it," Mrs. Marquez said solemnly.

"They'll find him. He'll be all right," Felicidad said, but her mind was sick with worry, and she tried to push from her thoughts the horrible visions that came to them. She was tormented by self-accusations. She was the one who should have taken care of Willy. Carlos was too busy with his work and Margarita, and her mother didn't know what was going on. She, Felicidad, should have stayed home, spent more time with Willy, and made sure that he didn't wander about and that he stayed away from whoever had given him that horrible shirt.

Abruptly she fled into his bedroom and lifted up the

mattress to see if the shirt was there. It was, with that sinister black arrow—like a snake—sharp against the whiteness, and for some unknown reason she felt a momentary sense of relief. But the feeling didn't last long. Perhaps Willy would be safer if he were wearing the shirt. Perhaps then he would be less vulnerable.

It was almost three o'clock when Carlos came back, white-faced and shaken. Yes, a patrol car had found Willy. He had been lying in an alleyway, beaten up, and they had taken him over to St. Vincent's Hospital.

The hospital was cool and clean and orderly, and the Sisters were kind and familiar. Felicidad and her mother and Carlos were allowed to see Willy for a few minutes, and the doctor assured them he would be all right. But he looked small and helpless in the white bed, his head swathed in bandages and his broken right arm in a cast.

"He must not talk yet," the doctor said. "He must stay very quiet."

The police officer was courteous and kind and said he would come back the next day and see if it was all right to question Willy. They wanted very much to know who had done this terrible thing.

Felicidad clung to her mother and to Carlos, and presently the three of them left and went to church and said a prayer for Willy. The priest came to talk to them, too. At first Felicidad felt very shy with this tall, somber-faced man, so different from Father Sebastian, but his voice was soft, and there was emotion in his face when he addressed them.

"This is a terrible thing," he said, his voice trembling slightly. "Children are getting killed on the streets. I wish I had a hundred arms and a hundred legs, so that we could do more than we are doing. But it takes time and patience and lots of work. Your child will get well," he said, patting Mrs. Marquez on the arm. "We will pray for him, and we will pray also for the day when this wonderful city will be a safe place for everyone to walk in freely, when no group will want to harm another."

Later he told them about his plans for a youth center in the neighborhood and for celebrating all the native Puerto Rican festive days. He said that many people and organizations in the city were working hard to get rid of the tenements and to build better houses and schools for the Puerto Rican families.

Felicidad listened attentively, but she knew that five or ten years from now would be too late for her. She wished that all these things were here *right now*. She couldn't wait that long. A thought was forming in her mind that she was aching to tell her mother and Carlos as soon as they were alone.

No one went to work that day, and in the afternoon when the Marquez and Esteves families were all gathered together in the kitchen, Felicidad, in a very quiet voice, dropped her bombshell.

"I think we should go home," she said to her mother. "I think we should move back to Barranquitas."

Everyone stared at her, and then everyone spoke at once. "We have to wait for Willy," her mother cried out.

"Of course. I meant as soon as he gets out of the hospital," Felicidad said.

"I don't want to go back there," Carlos said emphatically. "This is a fine place to live. I like it."

"How can you like a place where nobody likes you?" Felicidad turned to her brother angrily. "Where your brother gets beaten up by hoodlums, where it isn't safe to walk on the street, where you live like this!" Her eyes took in the broken plaster of the dark, dilapidated old kitchen.

Carlos shrugged his shoulders. "It won't always be this way. I can make more money up here in a year than I can make in three or four years at home. Besides,"— he boldly glanced across at Margarita—"Margarita and I have set the date for our marriage."

Carlos' announcement stopped the discussion for a while. Everyone kissed and hugged him and Margarita and each other, and Mrs. Esteves immediately started making plans for the wedding. Margarita would have a church wedding, of course, and they would hire a hall for a reception party. Mrs. Esteves even knew exactly the place to go for a wedding gown. She alternated between hugging and kissing Margarita lavishly, and scolding them, because this was a terrible way to announce their plans. "When poor little Willy is in the hospital!" she said.

Later Felicidad spoke to her mother quietly. "As soon as Willy is well enough, I think the three of us should go home. This is no place to bring him up. And I am homesick," she added simply. "I want to go home."

Her mother's eyes lit up. "I am homesick too," she agreed, and then her eyes clouded over. "But how can we live without Carlos to run the farm for us?"

She turned to her daughter helplessly, and Felicidad felt the burden of the decision resting on her. She knew that in the end, she would be the one to decide what to do and to make the necessary arrangements for doing it. It was still a strange feeling for her to have her mother depend on her for so much, but also in many ways she felt better prepared to take the responsibility than when they had first arrived in New York. For so long now she had been making her own decisions, about her job, about Willy, about Jim—about how she felt about everything.

She answered her mother thoughtfully. "I can work at home in Barranquitas. I'll find a job—maybe up at the Inn. And our cousin and his family can stay on in the house with us. With just the three of us, we can manage. Willy and I can help him with the bananas, and we'll have enough."

"But you wanted to be here for your future and for Willy's," her mother said.

Felicidad smiled. "You argued on the other side before," she said.

"Yes, I know." Her mother had a wry smile on her face. "But I want to make sure this is what you want, and I'm trying to think of you. I think maybe you are just upset because of that boy next door and because of Willy."

"I am," Felicidad admitted. "But I've been thinking about this before." There was so much she couldn't tell her mother—a million little things that in the re-telling would sound foolish and petty—all the little dis-appointments and the small sharp hurts and insults. But they added up to a feeling that grew the more she thought about them and about her desire to see Fer-nando. She did not feel at home here, and she was afraid she never would, not the way Carlos and Mar-garita did.

Their conversation was interrupted by a knock on the door. Felicidad opened it and was taken aback to find Jim standing there. He stepped inside, looking enormous in their low-ceilinged kitchen. He towered above Carlos and Mr. Esteves.

"I heard about your brother's getting hurt," Jim said, awkwardly shifting his weight from one foot to the other and glancing around at everyone with embarrassment. "I just wanted to tell you how sorry I am."

"Thank you," Felicidad said quietly, moved by Jim's coming to see her, but surprised at how quiet her heart was as she looked at him and talked with him.

Jim drew her aside. "And I want to apologize about the other night," he said. "I know you weren't fooled by it. It was my mother. I should never have let her push me around. Will you give me another chance?"

Felicidad smiled at him. "We're going home—my mother and Willy and I—as soon as Willy gets out of the hospital. We're going home to Barranquitas!" Her heart swelled with emotion at the words, "home to Barranquitas."

"Say, that's not fair. You've got to give us a chance! You haven't even seen New York yet. It's really a wonderful place."

"I've seen all I want to see," Felicidad said with a little laugh. "No, but seriously, I know it is a wonderful place, but it's not for me. I'll be happier at home."

"Can I see you before you go?" Jim asked anxiously.

"Certainly. We're not going so fast—not until Willy is O.K."

With so much happening, the rest of the day was tumultuous. For one thing, Mrs. Benton also came to see them. She, too, was full of concern and self-accusation. "We're all too busy with our own problems," she said to Felicidad and her mother, as she drank *café con leche* with them in the kitchen. "We forget about our neighbors. There are so many things I wanted to do for Felicidad—and Willy too. I wanted to take them over to the Settlement House, where they could have met some young people and had some fun, but it was one of those good intentions I never carried through. I hope you don't think too badly of all New Yorkers. We're in a hurry, and we're thoughtless, but we're not all bad!"

Felicidad assured her that she had been the kindest person of all to her. She wished she could explain better why she wanted to go home. It wasn't because she thought New York was bad, but she was homesick, and at home she felt more like a person in her own right. At home she was somebody, but here she was just another girl from Puerto Rico. It was difficult to explain to anyone.

The priest came to see them several times. He was very sympathetic and understanding about their wanting to go back to Barranquitas, but he also helped Felicidad get a more positive feeling about New York and to understand better its conflicts and its richness. The priest showed her all the letters in the newspapers and the articles, in both the Spanish and the English press, that represented the thousands of people who wanted to help the Puerto Ricans and to have them enjoy the city.

There was even a picture of Willy in some of the papers, and this time the stories were not a new hate wave against the Puerto Ricans. This time it meant that all those people and their organizations were extending their hands in friendship and help.

"New York is a very wonderful city," Father John said, "but it takes a long time for the Puerto Ricans to understand New York, and for New York to understand the Puerto Ricans. Their cultures are very different, and we all have to help bring out the best in both."

Felicidad read all the papers thoroughly, and tears came to her eyes, but her mind was still made up. For her and her mother and Willy it was best to go home.

Toward evening, when they went to see Willy again, he was sitting up in his bed eating his supper, and they could talk to him a little. He had received lots of presents from all their Puerto Rican friends and neighbors and from Jim and Mrs. Benton and even from strangers. He was surrounded by gifts and was all excited. "Isn't it great, Mama?" he cried when they came in. "Everyone's so nice to me!"

"I'd rather it hadn't happened," his mother said, kissing him and puffing up his pillows.

Willy said he had told the police officer he was pretty sure who the boys were that had beaten him up. They were members of the Black Arrow gang, who had been pressing him before to have nothing to do with Danny. Nothing in that neighborhood was a secret from them, and apparently they knew about Mrs. Marquez and Felicidad's visit to the police station. "They know everything that goes on," Willy said, "and I guess they found out that the Smiths were our friends, and they got mad. It was their way of getting even and warning me to stay away from Danny."

Mrs. Marquez was shocked by this news, but she said quietly, "I am sorry you were hurt, son, but I am not sorry I told them about Danny. I would do it again if I had to."

Felicidad hugged her mother hard when she said this, and she felt a great warmth envelop her. They would go back to their small village having learned a great deal by their experience of living in New York.

Chapter 16

❦

"I don't need this heavy coat," Felicidad said to Margarita. "You keep it."

She was busy packing, because the next day she and her mother and Willy were to board a plane to go back to San Juan. The soft, warm bathrobe, however, Felicidad lovingly folded in with her clothes. She'd never part with that. Always it would remind her of getting out of bed on those bitter-cold mornings and of the wonderful, comforting warmth it had given her.

Willy was out of the hospital and as good as new. He had been much relieved and very happy when he was told they were going home to Barranquitas. "No more of that jail!" he had cried joyfully, flinging his school-books up in the air.

Carlos and Margarita had been married in a beautiful wedding, and now Felicidad and her mother were anxious to be home in time for Good Friday, which was just a couple of days away. The apartment was jumping with excitement. Willy wouldn't part with any of his gifts, and his mother insisted they couldn't take all that baggage on a plane. Mrs. Esteves kept coming into Felicidad's room with other gifts that she wanted her to take back home and which Felicidad had no room for in her suitcase.

"I wish you were coming too," Felicidad said to Margarita, who was helping her.

"Carlos and I like it here. Carlos doesn't want to be a farmer, and here he makes good money. But we'll come back to visit," Margarita said, and added teasingly, "will you marry Fernando when you get home?"

"Maybe I'll find him married already. I'm no good at writing letters. I haven't written to him in ages, so I don't know how he feels about anything."

"He'll be the same Fernando, sticking on his farm, playing his guitar—he'll never change."

"I guess not," Felicidad agreed. She was afraid to think about Fernando. Would she feel the same about him? Or after New York, would he seem too much like an old-fashioned, simple village boy? And how would he feel about her? Would he be shocked if she told him she had gone out in New York unchaperoned?

Felicidad knew that she would never go back to exactly the same ways she had followed before she left Barranquitas. Her relationship with her mother had changed too much in this short time. Now she was used to having to make decisions, and she could not go backward to the child who had been so dependent on her

parents and on tradition. New ways didn't frighten
Felicidad any more, and she cherished her independ-
ence. It made her feel that she was bringing home
within her something positive and good from her trip
and from her experiences.

"It will be hard for you to go back home," Margarita
said intuitively. "You are a different girl, and you
won't like the old ways."

Felicidad nodded thoughtfully. "I've been thinking
about that. But little by little, things in Puerto Rico
are going to change too. I suppose," she added wisely,
"that every time a family comes home from the States
it changes a little bit more."

Their conversation was interrupted by Danny and
Mrs. Smith, who had come in to say good-by. Mrs.
Smith had gifts for Willy and his mother and sister to
show her gratitude for what they had done for Danny.
Mrs. Marquez received them graciously and was de-
lighted when Willy suggested that he leave for Danny
half of the presents he had been given in the hospital.
The two boys shook hands and said good-by solemnly,
and Felicidad felt a surge of emotion at the way the
eyes of the two mothers met over the dark heads of their
sons.

Their Puerto Rican neighbors and friends kept coming in to say good-by all afternoon. It was almost four
o'clock when Mrs. Benton came in. She was breathless
from the stairs. "I know it's awfully short notice," she

said to Felicidad, "but the truth is, I couldn't get hold of a baby sitter. However, my husband and I would like to take you out tonight. Can she come?" she asked Mrs. Marquez.

Mrs. Marquez smiled and said in Spanish, "I'm not the boss any more. You'll have to ask her."

Felicidad interpreted for her mother and said she'd love to go. Hastily, as soon as Mrs. Benton left, she dug out her good clothes from the suitcase and got dressed for the evening.

Promptly at six-thirty the buzzer sounded, and kissing her mother good-by, Felicidad flew down the stairs to meet the Bentons. She was surprised and excited to find that Jim was with them.

It was a glorious evening. This was the night Felicidad had dreamed of experiencing when they had first decided to come to New York. They went to an elegant restaurant, where they sat on deep, soft settees and ate foods Felicidad had never tasted before. She felt as if one of the magazine pictures had come true as she gazed around at the crystal candelabra lights and the beautiful women with their furs draped behind their chairs and listened to the soft music of a piano playing.

Mrs. Benton's face was beaming. "Are you enjoying it, Felicidad?" she asked.

Felicidad nodded her head. "It's beautiful."

Mrs. Benton sighed. "When the American tourists go to your island, so many of them see only the rich

Continental hotels. They don't really see the people or your beautiful landscape. And when your people come here, they see only the poor, dirty parts of New York. They don't see all the lovely places we have. It's a pity."

After dinner they went dancing at a night club, and she and Jim were on the dance floor all the time. "Do you have a boy friend back home?" Jim asked her.

Felicidad laughed. "I don't know. I'll have to find out when I get there."

"Will you write to me?"

"I'm not very good at writing in English, but I'll try." Then, with her eyes twinkling, she asked, "Which girl did you finally invite to that dance?"

Jim blushed. "I took your advice in a way—neither of them. I went without a girl." His eyes met hers, and they both laughed.

Felicidad hesitated before asking her next question, but she felt it was important for her to know. "Does your mother know that you are out with me tonight?" she asked softly.

Jim's eyes met hers. He nodded his head. "Yes, I told her."

Felicidad's eyes flashed, and she looked at him admiringly. "I am glad," she said simply.

Perhaps it was just a little grain of sand, but she felt proud that Jim had taken his stand. Yes, one day *Neuva York* would change too—there must be hundreds and hundreds of Jims in it. The thought was another private gift to take home, although she knew that an evening like this was a rare and isolated treat for a Puerto Rican girl like herself to enjoy.

It was a lovely evening, yet part of her inner excitement was in knowing that tomorrow they would be going home again, that tomorrow night she would be back in Barranquitas, in her own room, with the almond tree outside and the song of the *coqui* to sing her to sleep.

When the Bentons and Jim said good night to her at her door, there were tears in Felicidad's eyes. Mrs. Benton and Jim were her two very good friends, and she was sad at leaving them and proud, too, that in this big, strange city she had found two such fine friends.

The square in Barranquitas was sparkling in the brilliant sunshine. Every color stood out, sharp and clean—the dark hair and white dresses of the little girls, the older women in their somber black, and the myriad of bright colors on men, women, and children, everyone of whom, dressed in their finest clothes, had come from all the villages around to watch the procession on Good Friday.

Close by, so that she could almost reach out and touch them, were all her dearest friends: Pilarín, looking beautiful in a white piqué dress, with her family; Maria; Louisa; and all her schoolmates and sorority sisters.

"The people are all so beautiful!" Felicidad said to her mother. "I never really saw them before!" She felt as if the smallest breeze could lift her up and carry her off. There was such a buoyancy within her, a recognition and a love for everything familiar that she looked at—the candy store, the shoe store, the funny pink house where old Señor Rodríguez lived, the bright flowers, the trees, and the one special tree on the plaza where Fernando always used to sit after school, and where he was even now with his family, with his eyes smiling across at her.

He had come to greet her when they returned home, but so far, they had not had an opportunity to be alone together, what with all the excitement of her returning home and getting ready for the holiday.

Now she was busy with her mother, greeting all their friends and relatives—distant cousins who had come from other villages. This wonderful solemn day had a private and special meaning for her, almost as if it had all been arranged to welcome them home.

There was a hush over the square; the procession had started. The white coffin was carried aloft in a blanket of flowers. Those who marched came up behind slowly, their heads lowered in prayer, the women holding their rosaries in their hands. Somewhere a child let out a quickly hushed whimper. Everyone was quiet as all eyes turned toward the church, where the coffin was borne carefully up the stairs.

Felicidad had to close her eyes, because the beauty of the day and the love that filled her heart for Jesus on the Cross were more than she could bear.

Later, when they came out of church, Fernando was suddenly by her side. "Can we walk home together?" he whispered softly in her ear.

Felicidad nodded her head, and after a word to her mother, she followed Fernando through the crowds of people to the edge of the plaza. This was what she had been waiting for ever since she came home, and her heart was beating nervously.

"Not by the road," Fernando said, and taking her hand, he led her to the edge of the town, where a narrow donkey path zigzagged up the mountain to their homes. With a grin, Felicidad slipped her feet out of her good high-heeled shoes and gave them to Fernando to hold in his pocket. It was wonderful to be barefoot on the earth, to be able to dig her toes into the soft ground.

"I must look silly," she said, "in this dress, and barefoot!"

"You look beautiful," Fernando said. "How did you like New York? Tell me all about it. Did you go out with *otros muchachos en Nueva York?*"

Felicidad hesitated before she answered. She knew instinctively that she would not tell him, nor anyone, all about New York. She could never talk about the hurts and the anger and the resentments, about the dirt and the falling plaster and the *cucarachas*. Nor did she want to talk about the cold eyes of the ladies who interviewed her for jobs, nor Jim's mother, nor the looks from some of the people on the buses. So she told him about the good things—about Radio City and the big buildings and the fast elevators, about the beautiful shops and the fine restaurant where she had been taken to dinner and the night club where she had gone dancing the evening before she left.

"Why did you come home?" Fernando asked.

Felicidad's eyes met his, and then she smiled. "Because we were homesick—all of us, except Carlos. It is not all the way I tell you it is; it is not all a beautiful place for us Puerto Ricans. But Carlos and Margarita love it; they want to stay. I like it better here."

"I'm glad. I have news for you too," he said.

"What news?" Felicidad's eyes were bright, and her heart was pounding. What was he going to tell her?

"Hasn't anyone told you?" Fernando asked.

Felicidad shook her head. Was he engaged to be married? What other news could he have?

Fernando laughed. "Shall I keep you in suspense?" he asked teasingly.

"No! Tell me, please."

Fernando's dark eyes were shining in the sunlight, and Felicidad thought he had become even more handsome than he used to be. He looked very strong and self-confident. "Don't fall down from the shock. I have left the farm, and I am working in a factory. I study electronics at night." He watched her face eagerly, his own face proud with his news.

Felicidad was truly surprised. "But you said you hated factories! What happened?"

"It's a new factory, just outside the village," Fernando explained enthusiastically, "a beautiful factory, all windows—not dark and gloomy—everything the best, brand-new. I have a good job, and I am learning a great deal. And when I finish my studying I will get a fine job, right here at home. It makes me very happy."

"I am happy too. That is wonderful news, Fernando. I never thought you would change!" She laughed gaily. "I'll have to write to Margarita. She said you'd always be a farmer!"

"Everything changes. Even Puerto Rico. And I want more changes. I want you to be my wife, Felicidad." The words came out simply, as if they had been on his lips for a long, long time. They both stopped and faced each other, their hands clasped. "Will you?"

Felicidad looked into his eyes. "Of course. That is what I want more than anything in the world."

He took her in his arms and kissed her gently. Down below them the village was still gay with all the people in the square, and behind them the hills were green and purple in the sunlight. Now she was truly home where she belonged, in Fernando's arms, and Felicidad felt as if her past and her future had become one. She was filled with a nostalgic, almost sad awareness of the women who had gone before her—her mother, Abuelita, all the generations of women who had been asked these words, "Will you be my wife?"—and she felt a surging, wonderful ecstasy for the future.

"I love you, Felicidad." Fernando took her hand as they continued their walk toward home.

"I love you too," she said, her eyes on Fernando, but her heart also felt a love for the very earth on which they were walking.